PIYUSH THORAT

BlueRose Publishers

First Published in February 2021

ISBN: 978-93-5427-558-6

BLUEROSE PUBLISHERS

www.bluerosepublishers.com

info@bluerosepublishers.com

+91 8882 898 898

Cover Design:

Sanjay Shinde

Typographic Design:

Namrata Saini

Sketches:

Mayuri Satpute

Distributed by: BlueRose, Amazon, Flipkart, Shopclues

To Pam

To Pam

Home is where you are happy.

FOREWARD

It was an Induction Program for our new batch, on 27th July 2020. I took a session called "Building Self-Awareness" for my freshmen students of PGDM Batch 2020-22. After the session, I received several mails from students expressing how much they loved the session, one such mail was sent by a student "Piyush Thorat." He wrote, '*Good Afternoon Mam,*'

'Today's session regarding "Self Awareness" was really full of knowledge. And I have been very interested in this topic in my life and I read a few books about it, particularly about Stoic Philosophy. I have also read Dale Carnegie's books. I'd be very much obliged if you could kindly suggest some more books so that I can develop knowledge in this field. After all, you are a person of knowledge in this field and I do hope to learn many things from you.'

Little did I know that this one mail will start a string of meaningful conversations with my new student, a student in whom I saw immense potential, quest to know more, hunger to read more, gift to understand people's emotions and craft to tell stories. I was amazed knowing how many books he had read and how many were there on his to read list.

One fine day when he sent me a link to his blog, I realized this avid reader was an exceptional writer too. His story kept me intrigued and I could not stop myself from going to the next chapter after finishing one. I could see an August writer in him and was truly proud. A highly introverted person who struggles to express if you ask him a question in the class but the moment he has a pen in his hands, he transforms.

Since then, I have known Piyush really well. He writes to find solace, he writes to get peace, he writes to express himself and he writes to calm himself down and that's how this story came to be.

One night when he was feeling low and was unable to reach out to his friend Hrishi, who was then occupied with college submissions, he chose to write instead and hence the first blog was written. If Hrishi was available that time, maybe Piyush would have felt better just after speaking with him; and would have not bothered to write whatever crossed his mind.

But fortunately his friend was unavailable and he ended up writing till the dawn. Piyush's keyboard had churned out a beautiful piece that he posted as a blog, that called the attention of many readers. Who were intrigued by the story and demanded for the further chapters. Unplanned blog was now turning into a demand for answers and the number of requests kept growing. Until he finally decided to try to write further events. And he did.

Then after months, as he had come to my connection, shared with me that story and the first question I had after reading the story was: "*Why is it not a book?*" I am glad that I asked that as many had already. Now this is finally coming true.

I am ecstatic that in the process, he could write so many fictional events that it could take the form of a beautiful book. He is honest to his emotions and that is something, dear readers, that would connect you with the story. Be it David's challenges, struggles, dilemma, layered personality, his strained relationship with his father or the beautiful bond between David and Pam...you will be able to connect with the story.

Cheers!! To this one and many more.

- Prof. Shikha Sindhu

CONTENTS

CHAPTER 1
FREEDOM TO BE WEAK

David was returning from long day work. It was late and the neighborhood was asleep. Street dogs were staring at him as he was walking to his charmless house, until the street light showed his face dogs were defensive who had taken him for a thief but soon they ignored him.

David stopped at the front door of his house and took out keys from his pocket but he had half a heart to go back to home after his, another mundane day. He stayed there, lost in thinking. He sighed and then came out a little and looked towards the night sky. Pollution had taken away the beauty of seeing stars at night but the half-moon was lurking behind the grey clouds and was occasionally coming out to clear space of the sky. David looked to it with desperate hope, eyes misty and the heart was uneasy, like he was hoping something good will happen. He hoped that for a moment he wouldn't feel this sad.

But soon the clouds covered the beautiful sight of a half-moon and thus David looked down with failing hope. He stood there for a moment and then turned towards the door. He opened it and locked himself in his home. He went to his room, changed his clothes, and went to the kitchen for a bottle of water. In the dark kitchen, the light of the fridge was creepy but he was used to it all. He looked into the fridge and it was almost empty except with the stale food of last night and a couple of eggs and some water bottles. He picked one and went to his bedroom.

The noise of the droplet from the leak tap was haunting and loud at late night. David closed the door of his room and sat on the chair, opened a water bottle and drank lots of water and put the bottle with a snap on the table before him. He stayed idle in the same position for a while then put his both palms in despondence over his miserable face.

He broke down and he kept crying till his heartfelt little bit better, it was exhausted of the struggle he had to put every day to go on appearing normal. He finally took off his mask of that role, a role that he played all day long in front of people around him at his job. A role that he even had to play before his limited friends, with whom he didn't have a talk from the last few months, neither did they call to inquire about him. They were busy, that's what he often heard when he called them with high spirit and their such indifferent replies as well as dull tone only crushed his cheerful spirit of having a conversation with a friend.

David had a family, a drunken father and a controlling mother and he was separated from them since the days of his college. So no strings attached to them and neither was an option for him like most of the people to retreat to home when one felt empty and lost in life. All he had a small house of stark walls, walls looking as dejected and colourless as him.

He took out his phone and felt like calling her.

Jane.

The only person, who David had loved most and felt perfectly compatible with, until she cheated him with one of her friends. A woe ran through his heart as he remembered her face. It's been two years and yet the pain did not fade away. God, he missed how he was with her, how his life was when he was with her. He was filled with faith and strong as any man could ever be. He was happy......truly happy.

Tears had filled his eyes and he wiped them instantly. He went into the gallery of his phone and opened up one picture where she was in his arms and he felt so complete in his life. David felt numb suddenly and he stared at that picture blankly, without any emotion in his heart, just hollow.

And time passed like that until he was distracted by the sound of a loud thunder. It felt like it was about to rain. He picked up his earphones and lied on his bed. He put on earphones and played music on his phone, "*Cold by Jorge Méndez*". He was staring at the ceiling, listening to the music, feeling it deep in his heart while good, old, happy memories running in his head making him sad and happy at the same moment.

He heard Jane's voice in his head, coming from an old memory, she called his name, "David" and even in the memories he felt so good listening to her voice calling his name. His own name never sounded sweeter to him but when she would call it.

"*Why?*" he asked her while getting tormented with his good memories with her and had no answer. "*Why? I was so happy and then why did you do it to me Jane?*" and again tears were rolling down from his temples to the ears. He didn't bother to wipe them and just wanted to drown in his own sorrow that he was hiding. He just wanted this moment of freedom where he could feel his pain without any hesitation of being judged or mocked. He was a boy and he must act like a man, which is what he often heard from people around him. His mouth was often sealed in response and he kept asking himself, is it weak to be weak sometimes? There was some pressure society put on men to be strong, no matter how they feel inside. Not allowed to talk out their internal suffering and if they do, it often reflects as weakness, someone who can't handle emotional turbulence.

Often they hide their suffering in the fear of mockery. And act strong all day long, getting busy into work so that they will not feel these sad and tempting feelings of the past. Just running away and away and away, till life finally passes them by.

It had started to rain and the noise of rain in the background was only arousing more and more sad emotions with spirit for different kinds of happiness in them.

David changed the picture and saw Jane. She had just woken up from her sleep and still she was looking so beautiful and so delicate that she was covered in soft blankets and it was such a sight for David that he had captured such a moment in his phone's camera. He pulled up a blanket over him; it was getting cold as the night was passing by. He tried to feel the warmth of that blanket. It was the same blanket from the picture of Jane.

Later on as the music changed to "*Love and Loss by Mattia Cupelli*". The soft and deep sound of the piano was drowning David to his old memories with Jane. He saw one picture of her where she made stupid expressions looking at him. Showing tongue to the camera and closing eyes while doing so was making her look the cutest creature in the whole world. And in another moment David would remember how Jane was making an innocent face and big eyes just to get more affection from him. He would hug her and will always kiss her on her forehead making her feel that he's always there for her and would never leave her no matter what.

The truth was that David had learned to live his life by looking at Jane. Deprived of the happiness of family he had found his home with her and life was a waste for him if she was not with him in those moments. He would often keep looking at her when she would fall asleep in his arms. And arranging her hairs with his finger behind her ears was one of his favourite activities with her. Sometimes he would keep looking at her face for hours and keep asking himself that such a beautiful reality could be his? Dreaming about a beautiful future with her was his pastime activity.

A thunder strike disturbed him from his favourite chain of thoughts. He got up and walked to the window. Street light would be reflecting over the glass and the raindrops were making reflections vague and beautiful in that stormy night. Such Downfall had frozen his ability to be happy and the only way David could manage to feel happy is to go back to the good old memories with Jane.

Seeing through the window glass, all the vague displays had put his heart into a clear memory. Jane would often walk to the window holding a cup of coffee, wearing one of David's shirts. After sex Jane would often wear his shirts over her naked body and would often be in a playful mood. Sometimes she would just keep staring through the window thinking about life. And when David would see her lost in such thoughts he would gently come and give her a hug from behind and kiss her behind the ear.

"*I Giorni by Ludovico Einaudi*" played next to David's music player. And with the soft music of this Italian pianist he fell into the soft memories with his loved one. The Days as I Giorni means, he remembered those days when she would be affected with little things of David. If he was sick she would be worried and attentive to his needs. She'd make food for him and they both would have it together. Sometimes they would watch movies together and then with a connecting scene they would automatically find themselves holding each other's hands, assuring each other that they both were feeling the same thing at that moment.

Going out on walks and acting childish around David was Jane's favourite thing. She would often feel so protected in his arms and would say to him, that she feels most safe when he hugs her, and then David would tighten the hug just to make her feel safer and also give her a belief that she'll always be safe, because he'll be there.

David loved to be with Jane. She understood him and accepted him with all his strength and weaknesses. He would often open up his weakness before Jane and she would calmly listen to him and then give him a kiss and tell him that he can do it. He can face the challenges. Later on, he would be filled with tremendous confidence and he would pull off the challenges of the prevailing time. He would get vulnerable before her and would not feel embarrassed for doing so, and that was one of the best things David could feel around Jane, to not have to be strong all the time. He had freedom to be weak. He knew that she wanted to be there for him and hold him when he is feeling down. Then the next music played "*Touch by Mattia Cupelli*".

David was feeling down for real and then he suddenly realized that these are all memories. He's alone in that home and there is nobody but him. Jane is not there anymore, not even in his life. She's gone. This realization broke him down once again.

"*Oh Jane! Where did you go? Did you not know how much I really loved you? Yes, I am broken. Yes, I cry alone at night. Yes, I still need you despite what you did to me.*" And David started to cry out, taking out all his pain. Crying was not even enough to empty his pain. "*I'm vulnerable without you. Can't you see that I don't know how to live my life? All I ever lived, all I could ever understand was when I was with you. I was so happy, you know, I was even dreaming about family with you. And the foundation on which this relation was built: Trust; you broke it. You've hurt me and I have to keep acting that it doesn't affect me, but the truth is* IT DOES, EVEN AFTER ALL THIS TIME. IT FUCKING DOES." And then he kept sobbing.

After sometimes David wiped his tears; he knew that it didn't matter. Nothing really matters. He took a moment to process it and then prepared himself to wear that mask again which he will need for tomorrow's life, that same old mundane schedule, around the careless people HE must walk ahead, wearing a mask of a smile on his face.

Dante Alighieri, the Italian poet, once said it right that '*there is no greater sorrow than to recall happiness in times of misery.*'

When the heart is overwhelmed and scared of nothingness and unknown of the future, it tends to be romantically sad with past good memories just to abate the current suffering.

CHAPTER 2
TABLE FOR TWO

It was Saturday evening and David finally had made up his mind to get out of the home and spend his time differently: which was around the people. He didn't have any friends so he decided to take a walk alone. He thought to have dinner out in a restaurant after his walk to Brighton beach. So he got dressed up, blue jeans and white casual shirt along with black casual blazer and his brown oxford shoes, clean shave and well-groomed hair making him absolutely and a complete Classy British Bachelor. A man dresses up as it defines his character.

He planned to spend some time walking to Brighton Beach and probably would love to see the drowning sun from Brighton Pier. David chose to walk as it was three blocks away from his house as well as it will kill his most of the time and possibly exhaust him enough to fall asleep without putting much effort. For a long time falling asleep for him wasn't as easy as it was in childhood. Youth indeed takes away many childhood things.

As he was reaching Brighton beach he started to hear the seagull cry and clash of waves.

David took a sight of the clear and open space of the beach. Alas he wouldn't be getting a sight of the sun, blessing of the bleak climate of Brighton, and the seashore was making the vibes melancholic; which is exactly what David was trying to escape from but it appears he can't escape them even by accident. He put his hands in his pocket and started to walk quickly. As a weekend too many people had come out to spend their time with family and Brighton Beach was a common hang out place for Brighton people.

A main road was by the edge of the beach, and a special lane was for people taking a walk on that road. Considering the pattern, authorities had taken extra measures for securities for pedestrians which was making them safe from unexpected car accidents. As he was walking on that lane he was quite nervous around the people and trying to look down most of the time. Yet he had caught the eyes of many beautiful women who'd be standing by the edge of the lane, looking at the sea, and also those who were taking a walk on the same lane. David naturally avoided eye contacts with them, threatened that it will open up the doors to unsolicited conversations with strangers.

All these pretty faces and yet his eyes lingered on the face from memories and he did not know after everything that happened why he was still into such a situation.

David then walked to the beach, breathing salty air of the ocean and often looked up to the bleak sky covered in grey dull clouds. The lights on Brighton Pier were the only thing that felt lively enough to turn his direction towards itself.

On the pier families often came along, especially married couples with their children. It was also known as pleasure pier mainly because it had entertainment for little children to the elders. Elders often preferred to sit on the benches relishing a little period of peace and solace. David had grabbed himself one bench and was looking at the western horizon of the sea. Few young girls were also in Pier around David's position taking photographs for their Instagram posts and they noticed him but David didn't acknowledge their presence and enjoyed his own company. After spending enough time alone he had fallen in love with solitude and it was making him uncomfortable to socialize himself into someone's company.

After some time he noticed a little girl with blue eyes and dark hair, wearing a unicorn puffy hat, holding fingers of her parents with her both hands and taking her small steps on Pier. This beautiful sight brought a smile on David's face, maybe no matter how depressed a man is in his life, a sight of little kids is enough to bring a smile on his miserable face.

David looked at that family for a while observing how happy they all looked together. There was some colour in their lives which he himself lacked in his own: Love.

He felt good for a while looking at that little happy family until the sight was seizing his heart again with melancholic feelings of past desires. When it became unbearable he stood up, not understanding that the girl who was about to approach him was startled a bit and was now reevaluating her choice of whether to approach him or not. But David started to walk off the Pier discarding any validation for that girl's presence and now was heading to the restaurant called La Capannina, a classic Italian restaurant.

After a 20 minutes walk, he finally reached the restaurant. As he entered one of the waitresses approached him.

'Table for two, signor?' she asked. She was really pretty.

David was lost for second in some trance and then he quickly handled himself back to the present moment.

'Um... No. No... it's just me.' He fought really hard to not think about Jane at this moment.

'Very well, signor.' replied the waitress. 'This way.' She was leading him to a vacant table.

David saw that the table was in the middle and lots of tables were circulating it, which he felt rather uncomfortable. He said hesitatingly to the waitress, 'Um... excuse me.' She looked back at him.

'Could you please suggest a place which is more, um, secluded than this one where I wouldn't be disturbed by the ..... crowd.'

The waitress observed him for a moment and then quietly headed towards a table near the window, where a light was falling over the table and had a blue vibe about it. 'This is a Table for Two and I guess you are two so that wouldn't be an issue.'

David was confused with the answer. 'I beg your pardon.' he exclaimed.

'Signor,' the waitress answered calmly, 'a man demands this kind of table on two occasions, one he has a date with the love of his life and second when that love of his life is in his memories and he wants to miss her without any disturbances.'

David was surprised by the possibility that there could be some strangers who might understand him better than those who knew him for years.

'Have a seat, signor.' the waitress pulled out a chair for David. He blankly sat on it and then looked at the waitress. She was waiting for him to order and David had lost track of the event and was into a confused state of heart and mind and was stuck into the blank stare.

'Signor?' the waitress demanded.

Snapping out of the thoughts David said, 'Yes?'

'Your order?'

David had lost his focus and was looking into the menu without any clue. Seeing to his trouble, the waitress interrupted.

'Pardon me, signor.' David looked at her. 'If you'd like to have my suggestion, why don't you just order what SHE liked?'

David looked at her for a moment incredulously and then he felt the idea was quite thoughtful. It had spared him from the hectic effort of choosing the food he would not know that he'd really enjoy but still had to take a chance. It was better to order the familiar item than trying out something new.

'That is quite thoughtful.' replied David.

'So what did SHE like?'

David smiled to himself and answered, 'She would often eat pizza...'

'Which one?'

'Margherita' The waitress smiled. David noticed that but still continued, 'Siciliana. Both regular size and put extra olive on Siciliana. She used to love that a lot.'

'Quite some choice.' replied the waitress with a smile. 'Anything else?'

'Torta Al Cioccolato was her favourite which she often preferred to eat at the end.'

With a smile on her face, the waitress asked for drinks.

‘Well she used to drink beer with it, which I can't order.’

‘Why?’ asked the waitress curiously. The restaurant did have one of the finest beers available.

‘I don’t drink.’ answered David. ‘So *Cuba Libre* would be fine for me along with pizza. That would be all.’

‘Perfect couple.’ The waitress whispered to herself.

‘I beg your pardon.’ demanded David.

‘She appears to be a childish, talkative and stubborn kind of girl and you are a serious, mature and lacking love type of gentleman.’

David was bewildered. ‘How do you figure that out, from the choice of food?’

‘Signor, a person is not merely defined by the kind of dress one wears but also the kind of food he/she prefers. Years of experience and family business teach these things at an early age.’ answered the waitress. ‘I’ll be back with your order in 20 minutes, till you can enjoy your desolation, Inamorato.’

David looked at her for a couple of moments while she was going and then suddenly wondered what she called him. But he then restored back to his usual mindset. He thought for a while he was really distracted from them and had a new kind of sensation about it which, on the contrary, he did like.

'Here's your order, signor.' that waitress came along with two pizzas.

'Thank you.' said David. As the waitress was going back David felt an uncontrollable urge to profess her one thing. 'Hey...' he said exasperatingly. She turned back to him and looked at him attentively. David spoke off, 'Well... just to be clear, um, she wasn't that childish. She was the very mature girl I'd ever known.'

For a moment the waitress mull it over and replied, 'As a girl I can tell you one thing.'

'Which is?' David said quite curiously.

'A girl is often reserved and mature in general but only acts childish around that boy to whom she really feels in love with.' David felt Jane for a moment in his heart. 'But I wonder what could possibly be the reason that she's not with you.' That changed David's expressions to a serious note. 'I'm sorry I didn't mean to pry.'

'It's okay.' replied David serenely.

Seeing the expressions of David the waitress said, 'Signor if you'd like, I can play her favourite music over the system, that will unburden my guilt of intrusion over your privacy.'

David chuckled. 'On the contrary....Ms...' David paused. He didn't know her name. He looked at her questioningly. 'I'm sorry I don't know your name.'

Waitress smiled gently and answered, 'Vanessa.'

'I'm David.' he was then quiet for a moment. 'So Vanessa, you didn't intrude on my private thoughts. On the contrary, I felt good talking with you. It's been really long with whom I could talk a little.'

'What about your friends?' wondered Vanessa.

'I don't have any. I'm new here in Brighton.' answered David.

'Oh! I see. So that's why you are.... alone?'

David chuckled, 'No. We indeed had a break-up. It's not that distance had separated us.'

'Can I ask you what her name was?' asked Vanessa so curiously.

'Jane.'

'That's a pretty name. I am sure she was as pretty as her name.'

'She was.' David proudly confirmed that.

Vanessa smiled looking at David. 'Well I must get going with my work.'

'Yeah.' responded David. He didn't feel good losing such an interesting company but he knew that the obligation of work often crushed our little tempting desires. To David's surprise, he desired in his heart to be a friend with Vanessa if he could.

'I almost forgot, which song would you like to listen to while you enjoy your meal, signor?'

'Bruno Mars was Jane's favourite, I guess his "It will rain" song shall define me right now.'

'Very well, signor.' Vanessa turned back to the counter.

David set himself comfortably and started to have his meal and enjoy the moment of solitude. After a minute the song played gently over the music system of the restaurant. David looked at the counter where Vanessa was. She looked at him and smiled. David also exchanged a smile and then looked out of the window. The dusk was covering the light of the ocean and he was falling into the memories once again.

CHAPTER 3
A NEW FRIEND

Next day David was feeling vigorous than usual and there was some glow over his face. He was enthusiastic and got up early on Sunday morning. He had gone for a run on Brighton Beach and was returning back to his home on Blaker St.

On his way back to home, over St. James st, he was noticing the neighbourhood which he often avoided because of his preoccupied sad thoughts. Something cheerful was sparkling from within him. His face was joyful and eyes were confident. Today the sun had come out and was making the morning quite cheerful, paths were almost empty and shining with sparkling windows of the shops around it. As he was observing shops while running, he was about to clash on the sky-blue bicycle which was coming from the Madeira PI st. At the intersection a girl was trying to cross to St. James st.

'Woooah!' David was panicked as his attention fell on the bicycle ahead of him. He was so fast that he had to jump from the front tire of the bicycle but his leg had hit the edge of the basket. He looked behind, the girl was also scared and had almost closed her eyes in the panic of the clash. 'Are you okay Ms.?' David said. A girl in her mid-twenties wearing a Blue Denim Pinafore dress, over a white top, half sleeves till the elbows, making her look absolutely pretty and intensely desirable.

'Are you going to create wanton destruction on the road for the revenge of your broken heart, David?' The girl said mending her basket on a bicycle.

David was perplexed and took a good look at her face. For a moment he couldn't recognize her. She was looking so beautiful that he could not think for a moment that this girl was his waitress last evening in that Italian restaurant.

'Vanessa?' he uttered in surprise.

'Nice to see you.' said Vanessa in her casual wry remark.

For a moment David was numb and had lost his grasp on the present moment then he replied, 'Nice to see you too, Vanessa.'

She climbed down from her bicycle and started to take a walk holding her bicycle along with her.

'Where are you going?' asked David.

'It's Sunday morning I have to get flowers for restaurant decoration and afterwards I'm free to spend my day.' answered Vanessa.

'Not a holiday from work even on Sundays?'

'Especially on Sundays there is workload.' Vanessa answered, which had created a few questions in David's heart. 'You must be wondering when would I be getting holidays as a waitress?'

'Well, I guess everyone deserves good holidays.'

'But not everyone gets to spend their weekends as a holiday. Sometimes work hunts that little pleasure too. But I decided to live my time so I said to my father that I'll not be working on Sunday even if customers mob before the restaurant.'

'Wait a minute. If you want a leave, then how can you talk about it to your father instead of your employer?'

'Um... because my father owns that restaurant?' Vanessa answered.

'Oh! Right. That makes sense.' David said to himself.

'I guess I had mentioned to you that it's a family business, but then I can't expect you to remember such tiny details. Your mind was already preoccupied with Jane's thoughts.'

David laughed a little over that nag, 'That's true.' Vanessa smiled and headed towards the same direction of David.

'Where are you going?' asked David.

'To the florist before New Stein st.' replied her.

'Oh! That's a block ahead from Chapel st.'

'You live on Chapel st.?'

'No, I live on Blaker st.' said David. 'Via Chapel st. to Blaker st.'

'I see.' Vanessa kept walking.

David was also walking along with her but he was hesitating to and thought to ask her, 'Do you mind if I walk along with you till Chapel st?' a little panic lingered over David's face, thinking he would get refusal.

'I guess that's why I am walking by my bicycle instead of riding it.' A charming nag from Vanessa felt agreeable to David. He smiled and joined her.

'I guess so.' he said.

'So what do you do, David?'

'I work in RockLand Corporation as a Financial Analyst.'

'Ah! Smart guy.' said Vanessa.

'Not really.' David said feeling hesitant, 'It's... I don't know.'

'Just allow yourself some credit. At least sometimes.' said Vanessa. David just pressed his both lips and suppressed the smile over this slight compliment. 'Do you enjoy this job or you are doing it for money?'

'I always loved Economics so I do enjoy my job and money is fine.'

'How much do you make?' said Vanessa, then she suddenly realized that it's indecent to ask about income in England. 'I'm sorry I shouldn't have asked that. It's none of my concern.'

'Yeah, it's okay. I make fifty thousand pounds a year.'

'Fifty thousand?' Vanessa was shocked, 'That's some sizable amount. Well that defines your good taste in clothes and that huge tip you had left last evening.'

'Well you had made my evening special so...'

Vanessa smiled and she kept her eyes straight on the road. David was looking at her for a while.

'What about you?' asked David.

'Well, I have finished my Engineering, three years ago. Later on, I worked as office manager for a couple of years and then quit it. And for nearly a year I'm back to my hometown.' answered Vanessa.

'Why did you quit the job? Didn't enjoy it or wanted to do something else?' asked David.

'Actually, I had lost my interest in such a job. After enough thinking I finally came to the conclusion that I need a break to make a choice.'

'I am fascinated how you hide it well under your smile. Someone like me could not detect or think at a glance, that you could have such troubles too.'

Vanessa smiled and then looked at David and asked, 'So what brought you to Brighton? You are not from here, are you?' seeing the expressions of his face Vanessa guessed what answer she might be receiving, 'Don't answer that it was your job, I know you could have done it in London and earned a lot more than you do now. So what is it? Jane?'

'Well... um..' David was hesitant and confused how to talk about it. He wasn't used to such inquiry from someone. 'I guess she is a considerable reason for me choosing the Brighton.' and then laughed to himself.

'What happened?' asked Vanessa, wondering what could have possibly made Jane leave a guy like David. 'If you don't mind me asking it.'

David chuckled over the funny fact how Vanessa was curious to know yet she was contained by the proprieties. 'Well... someone else came into her life and then she fell in love with that guy while still being in a relationship with me.'

'Oh! I'm sorry.'

'It's okay. It happens. She used to tell me that he was her friend so I didn't have much doubt about it. I used to feel proud that how much I trusted her but then it turns out it was nothing but my stupidity.' he chuckled. 'Trust had blinded me from her many activities.' David answered and stopped for a moment, thought that he'd look weak if it seems that it still hurts him. He just tried to be cool about it. 'But it happens to everyone, I'm not spared from this either. So what's there to make a fuss about anyway?'

'But that still doesn't mean it won't hurt.' Vanessa looked at David. 'Recurrence of affliction on everyone does not mean it can't or shouldn't be felt individually.'

David had fixed his eyes on Vanessa for a couple of moments. It was true. It was hurting him badly and he had tried to talk about it to his friends but all they did was to make fun of it instead of understanding his pain or at least validating its existence. They all kept saying to him that it happens with everyone. He felt that hole of deficient comprehension had finally been filled by Vanessa.

'I'm surprised to see that you didn't joke about it. Break-ups have become a joke rather than heartbreak these days.'

'They have. I've had one for myself too.'

David looked curiously at her.

'Come on, can't I look like a girl who'd had a failed relationship in her past?' Vanessa joked to her own.

David was quiet for a moment trying to arrange his words, 'No... it's just... you don't look broken.'

'We all are broken in our life David, and we are constantly in practice of hiding it better than others. You hide it in your work. I, under my smile.'

'Are you still broken by your past? Of your broken dreams and desires?' wondered David.

Vanessa took some moments before speaking and then she finally spoke in her tired confident voice. David suspected that she also battled inside but chose to not show. He thought what a strange time we all live in, we all are dying because of something inside yet are unable to vocalize it. Our greatest fear these days is not being understood by someone the way we need to be understood.

'Sometimes I miss him,' spoke Vanessa 'as you did Jane last evening. I used to think about it a lot that we both could have had it all but it didn't work out, and for what? Nothing but he was afraid of the commitments. But I am healed and such reminiscent moments are quite rare in my life now. Maybe someday I will get back to my old profession.' Vanessa said hopefully.

'I have to deal with such moments daily. At night it becomes such an excruciating curse and I just can't sleep.'

'Did you sleep well last night?' asked Vanessa.

'In fact, I did and that was such an unusual thing. I must confess that it was, often, so difficult for me to fall asleep at night but last night I fell asleep as soon as I lay on the bed.'

'You're welcome.' said Vanessa in jest.

'Oh! You think it had your contribution to it?'

'Well we do make good and delicious food. Nothing gives you a good sleep as delicious food, Signor David.'

'Please just call me David, at least outside your restaurant. I understand in the restaurant it's your job and you have to maintain certain norms and follow rules but outside we are...' and David stopped.

'...Friends?' asked Vanessa, still looking ahead on the road.

David was looking at her, 'I mean friends.....like an acquaintance... you know... like that.'

Vanessa laughed and said, 'You do live by proprieties a lot, don't you?'

'Maybe.' David felt a bit embarrassed.

'We are almost at Chapel st.' said Vanessa.

'Oh!' David felt disappointed and sad. He could not notice how the time had passed. 'I guess here we part.' David stopped to the corner of Chapel St.

'I guess so.' Vanessa stopped a couple of steps ahead of David. She looked back at him.

'I guess here we both say goodbye.' said David.

'Goodbye?' said Vanessa, 'Aren't you hopeful that we'd see each other again?'

David smiled heartily. 'I don't think such pleasant coincidences will always occur in my life that I run into you unless I come again to your restaurant.

'You never know.' said Vanessa smiling coyly.

David burst out in laughter. He nodded his head and thought let's see how fate again crosses their roads.

'Right.' said he, 'I guess there are pretty much chances of that.'

Vanessa laughed heartily along with him.

'Maybe we can be friends then if you tell me more about Jane.'

David smiled and nodded in response.

'Okay then.... bye.' said Vanessa walking ahead to a florist shop.

David waited there to see her go. He was feeling something good inside, some new emotional budding was developing inside him. He then continued his run on Chapel St till he reached his home.

He spent his day making preparation for his new project at the company. His day went well and there were no sad and melancholic thoughts bothering to his peace of mind. David focused on his work and was excited for tomorrow.

CHAPTER 4
THE SYMPOSIUM

[Next Day: Monday]

David walked into RockLand Corporation's office. He was in a great mood and people were noticing something different about him. Usually grim-faced David was looking lively today.

'Hi David.' a colleague from his office greeted him. She was such a gregarious person.

'Hello Sarah.' replied David indifferently.

'You are looking different today.' she said while observing him meticulously which David didn't much like. Sarah often tried to figure out things of David which he tried to hide and her such inquiries were nothing but encroachment under the name of socialization. He didn't much like someone trying to get close to him in his office. He was quite professional and tried to keep things agreeable with almost everyone. Performing a lot better than his colleague had brought him the position of prerogative employee.

David did earn jealousy as he had earned a good name as a dedicated employee to the company and had earned a good designation. Matthew, his boss, was always pleased with his work and respected him for his attitude towards the work. But many suspected in office that David was not actually into his job, his real interest lied somewhere else, yet he was performing better than most of them combined, that had brought jealousy against him but nobody could dare to express it.

'What do you mean looking different today?' inquired David.

Sarah was confused yet pleased to see David in such a phase, 'Happy.' she answered.

David kept looking at her for some moment. Covered in his own pain, not allowing anyone in his personal space, minding his own business and taking out all the frustration or pain of whatever that was there in his life over his performance in the job. And such comments had only implied to him that something is changing with him. He wondered if the walls he had built were failing to protect him?

'Today there's a meeting with a valuable client of this company...I am just excited as I am well prepared for that meeting.' He killed the implication instantly which Sarah felt a few minutes back. She had gone to the wrong perception about him that she had convinced herself. After all, he was David.

'If you don't mind, could you excuse me please?' he put a smile after his question which made Sarah to excuse him with half a heart. She had no question, yet felt like asking something more.

David walked ahead to his cabin, exchanging polite nods with people in his office.

'Do you think he's married?' asked Olivia, another girl from the office.

'Do you see any ring?' asked Sarah.

'No.'

'So he isn't.' Sarah was still staring at him, observing how he was putting all his attention only in work in his glass cabin.

'But is he dating someone?'

'Who David?' the colleague was amused. 'He is the kind of guy who never allowed any woman to come close to him.' she spoke out of her failed efforts.

'Then he must be in a long-distance relationship.'

'Have you ever seen anyone this committed in LDR?'

'Then?' wondered Olivia.

'I suspect his heart was broken. He often seems in pain and puts all his focus on work and is less involved in other activities.'

'Other activities?'

'Like...partying, going out or even dating anyone for time being. He's kind of a serious guy. He doesn't much find meaning to the things that normal people do...there's nobody even here that can connect to him well, but he tries to be agreeable with everyone.'

'Tries?'

'I don't think he likes anyone here....not much.' said Sarah. 'I'd be surprised if anyone could talk with him for more than 2 minutes.'

'Why is that?' wondered Olivia.

'He doesn't allow anyone to open him up, neither does he himself.'

'Oh dear Sarah...maybe you'd not be able to appeal his interest. Ever.' and Olivia laughed over it. Sarah made a face and walked back to her table.

[The Evening Party After The Meeting]

Everyone was well dressed for the party. The party was hosted for a big client of the company and Matthew, the boss of David, wanted to do everything to please the client and get his approval for the next big deal. The meeting was satisfactory for a client and had chosen to go with the deal and Matthew predicted the same, that's why he had scheduled a party for the client.

'Oh I despise these rich brats, avarice for more wealth despite their already possessed opulence. And their mark over everything...their cars, their homes and swimming pools...god damn near everything. They act like they are some sort of trade name.' Jacob, an employee from the office talked while looking at the rich client from Manchester. Mr Collins the guest of the party.

David was his usual quiet in the parties. He didn't enjoy parties and thought they were unnecessary extravagances. Yet he had to put up with all the activities as a part of his job.

'You don't think that people like us do have such behaviours?' spoke David to Jacob while looking at Mr Collins. 'We are agreeable just because our desires are constrained by the lack of money. If he had the same amount of money as them, then we'd have, probably, behaved the same.' stated

David. Jacob seemed to have a difficult time to agree with him though he knew David was right. 'We are not so much different from them.'

'Matthew says that this deal could be so lucrative for the company.' said Philips, a skinny tall man in his thirties.

'Might we expect some bonus then?' wondered Jacob.

'Maybe.' said Philips. 'Only if Matthew doesn't use the money to buy himself a new car.'

'Then you better be on the team of our company which will be working for Mr Collins.' spoke Philips.

'I hope to get on it.' Jacob said ambitiously while his stare was still fixed on Mr Collins' hot wife.

'What about David?' wondered Philips.

'That guy would be already in the team. The way he explained his analysis, the client was impressed.' said Jacob. When he didn't get any response from David he finally broke his long lingering stare on Mrs Collins and checked for David but he was already gone from there. Both Jacob and Philips looked at each other and wondered where David would have gone but soon they both shrugged it off and focused back on Mr Collins' wife.

David had come into the gallery of that party hall. Came out for fresh air and particularly for some solitude. The topic of another man's wife was unbearable for him. And he didn't understand why would Jacob keep his eyes fixed on Mrs Collins while he was already married. Never be the third person in the relations of two and disrupt it. He thought of Jane and felt a pang in his heart until he was disturbed by a waiter.

'Drinks sir?' asked the waiter.

'Could I have some water?' asked David.

The waiter felt a bit strange but he simply nodded and spoke, 'Sure sir.' and then went off to get David a glass of water.

Meanwhile, David stayed there and was observing the view from the gallery until his eyes fell upon Sarah and other colleagues from the office. All of them were drinking wine, scotch, whiskey or champagne and smoking cigarettes. He looked at them for a second and narrowed his eyes in contempt and scoffed on them and looked the other way. Men drink to show their masculinity and women to show they are equal to men and both of these sorts of people were vain and contemptible in David's eyes.

Olivia was walking towards David and pretended like he didn't notice her. She came right before him and spoke nothing and kept staring at him for a moment or two. He got a bit confused and was silent in response too.

'David.' spoke Olivia staring straight to his eyes. He looked nervously here and there.

'What?' he asked hesitantly. He thought maybe she would ask him for the dance which he clearly wasn't ready for.

Seeing the hesitation of David, Olivia smiled and spoke, 'Matthew was asking for you.'

'Matthew?' David was a bit surprised. 'Okay.' and then the next moment he was walking towards his boss, ignoring Olivia completely. She noticed it and kept staring at him for a long time till he disappeared into the crowd.

As David reached there he saw that Matthew was along with the client: Mr Collins and his wife. It seemed like Matthew wanted David to meet Mr Collins.

'You asked for me, Matthew?' asked David.

'Yes...David.' Matthew spoke enthusiastically. 'I want you to meet Mr Collins, the El.Tech Corporation. They wanted to have a word with you.'

‘With me?' David was taken aback and then he looked at Mr Collins, a man in his late forties.

‘Hello young man. That was such an impressive presentation and analysis you made in the meeting. I must confess that I was impressed as well as convinced to go with your company with this deal.' spoke Mr Collins convinced.

David felt diffident and spoke, ‘Thank you, sir. That's so kind of you to say that to me.'

Mr Collins was impressed with David's mannerism. He noticed that David stood there empty-handed while everyone held a glass of champagne or wine. ‘Where's your glass, young man?' asked Mr Collins.

David looked at Mr Collins, smiling gently as he was amused over his question. ‘I don't have to as I don't drink, sir.'

Mr Collins was surprised to hear that. ‘You are a young man.' said Mr Collins. To which David chuckled lightly. ‘It's a good thing that you don't, but while we all are holding a glass of champagne or wine in this Symposium, you seem to be a misfit with your empty hands.'

Everyone along with David laughed over it. ‘The Symposium, you say sir?' asked David.

'Yeah.' said Mr Collins.

'As in like old Greece times of Plato and Socrates?' and David chuckled and he soon indicated a waiter to come for an order.

'Have you read The Symposium?' wondered Mr Collins.

'The 2400 years old work of Plato? Yes, sir.' answered David with a smile of pleasure. The waiter came and he gave an order, 'One Virgin Mojito, please.'

'It's good to see that I meet young people who have an interest in reading.' admitted Mr Collins.

'He's really fond of people who read.' spoke Mrs Collins. Mr Collins smiled at her and she did the same.

'It's good to know that Mrs Collins.' spoke David with a pleasant smile and a polite nod. 'Is it the reason why Mr Collin had found his love of life? His better half?'

Mr Collins smiled with pleasant happiness. 'I fell in love with her the moment I saw her reading that poem.'

'Which poem? We all wonder, sir.' spoke Matthew taking keen interest.

'Roads not Taken.' spoke Mr Collins.

'Robert Frost.' spoke David.

'Yes.' said Mrs Collins.

The waiter came with David's order and he picked up his glass of Virgin Mojito and smiled at everyone. 'I guess the gap is filled.'

Mr Collins laughed heartily. 'Matthew, I like this guy. I want him on the team.'

'He's already in the team, sir.' answered Matthew seeing his actions were getting successful.

'Matthew is really a good leader, Mr Collins.' Mr Collins gave his attention fully to the words of David. 'He gives opportunities for new people to rise and reach their potentials.'

'Very good Matthew. That's the quality of a true leader.' said Mr Collins, impressed with the words of David.

Matthew felt appreciated and could barely control his happiness. 'Thank you, sir.' David saw how the spotlight was properly shifted to his boss. He smiled and thought that he averted the possibility of jealousy from his boss.

'Very well then, so what is the topic of tonight's symposium?' wondered Mr Collins.

Everyone seemed confused and were thinking to suggest one good topic but all the ideas they thought didn't seem good enough.

'Socrates had the topic of Love at his symposium.' spoke David.

'Then shall we keep the same for ours?' wondered Matthew.

'That would be really engrossing.' said Mr Collins. 'So what is the situation of Love in today's world? Does it still exist? Is it still relevant?'

'I think it is still relevant.' spoke Sarah, who was quiet for all the time. Everyone wanted to participate in the conversation which was finally inclusive.

'I think it doesn't exist anymore.' spoke Philips. Many nodded to it showing their accordance.

'People struggle to find it and yet end up with not finding it.' spoke Jacob.

'I think one must love another person in order to be loved in return.' spoke Matthew.

'That doesn't happen in today's world. People love and yet their love is not reciprocated.' spoke Sarah. David couldn't agree more with her but he maintained his silence. 'But still, it is relevant.' she added.

'You young man, you seem to be quiet on this topic?' asked Mr Collins. 'Are you married?'

David chuckled and then replied, 'Marriage? That's the contract I don't want to sign, sir.'

'You think marriage is a contract?' asked Mrs Collins.

I beg your pardon, Ma'am. I didn't mean to offend.' said David politely.

'You certainly haven't, but I must say I am amused.' admitted Mrs Collins. 'What brings you to that conclusion?'

'Well, the simple observation is that in order to have a successful marriage, both sides must have something to offer each other that will sustain the marriage.' answered David.

'And what else there should be to offer than love?' wondered Mrs Collins.

'Money.' spoke David gently.

Everyone in the hall was amused and nodded in accordance. Even Mrs Collins seems to agree partly but she still believed that love is what makes the successful marriage.

'But aren't those with great riches also unhappy in marriages?' questioned Mrs Collins.

‘That's right too.' supported Matthew. ‘People with lack of money and with money are both, eventually, unhappy in marriage; yet in both the cases there are people who seem to be completely happy too. Why is that?'

‘Because money doesn't really buy love.' spoke Mr Collins. ‘It is an imperative part of life, I'll agree, but it shall not buy true love.'

‘Then why do people choose people with money?' questioned David. Some pang inside him was almost visible but soon he controlled and hid it well.

‘Because it buys comfort.' answered Mr Collins. ‘People these days are looking for comfort in life, as they are already miserable for many things. The slight comfort in someone's company is misunderstood as love...or maybe these days everyone craves for love but nobody understands how to value love...how it is acquired.'

‘Sir, do you still think that the way Zeus had cut off humans in half, they are still looking for that better half?' questioned David.

‘Zeus did what?' spoke Sarah.

‘In The Symposium by Plato' spoke Mr Collins, ‘there's a tale of Zeus separating humans. It was said that "According to Greek mythology, humans were originally created with four arms, four legs and a head with two faces. Fearing their power, Zeus split them into two separate parts, condemning them to spend their lives in search of their other halves.'

'Why did the mighty Zeus do that?' asked Sarah.

'Because the humans were attacking on Gods and Zeus was forced to split them in half as a punishment to humans. Now each human is looking for his/her better half even today.' spoke David. Mr Collins seemed pleased with David's knowledge in old content of philosophy.

'And do you think people do find their better half?' asked Mr Collins.

'Some do, most fail.' admitted David.

'Why do they fail?'

'Because they lack commitment or they fail to choose the right person.' said David confidently. 'Life as well as all sorts of relationships are full of challenges but most people think it's better to leave than to repair the relationship. This generation is choosing what is easy over what is right. Besides, we are living in a world where we have multiple choices so...' David stopped speaking.

'I shall agree with David there, when there are turbulent times people choose to leave and find other options.' spoke Philips. 'This picture can be seen in our day to day life too.'

'I think we must choose the one who chooses us, under all the circumstances.' Mrs Collins spoke confidently and looked at her dear husband. They both exchanged smiles.

'Most of us will be envious of you two seeing this much in love for such a long time.' spoke Matthew. 'You both make such a wonderful couple.'

And everyone cheered to that, even David. He was just so pleased to see that the ideas of love and people holding on each other are still a reality.

Mr Collins came to David and spoke to him, 'I hope someday you shall find your better half.' Mr Collins spoke with great hope in his eyes. David felt good and bad at the same time.

'That's very kind of you to say, sir. But I think I shall never find anyone as I can't feel connected with anyone.' spoke David.

'And why do you think that?' wondered Mr Collins.

'The thing is, I stay alone because I really don't enjoy the company of anyone. The people, I think I'd really enjoy being around, are all in the books and are in the old times. Sometimes it gets really difficult for me to cope with today's world when all that is filled in my heart are values of old times.' explained David.

Mr Collins laughed heartily to that and put his left palm on David's right shoulder. 'You are definitely going to find that one and it will be such an interesting story.' David pressed his lips in response. He didn't much agree with it but he nodded to Mr Collins. 'Now you must excuse me as I want to dance with my better half.'

'Sure sir.' David smiled and looked at Mr Collins. He walked to Mrs Collins like she meant all the world to him and asked her hand for the dance. She still acted like she was in her college day. That attitude and aura around her was still intact. David felt such a great delight looking at them and he genuinely smiled for this moment. Then slowly a glimpse of Jane troubled him in his heart. He missed how he was dancing with her then all her stupid moves in that home. David missed so much to Jane and felt pain in his heart. He had money, respect and things a young man needs in life...but not love. It was still not there in his life.

Seeing David stood there like that, Olivia came forward and spoke to him, 'David.' he felt disturbed from his thoughts. 'I was wondering...would you like to dance with me for the next song?' Olivia, such a sweet girl.

David looked at her and spoke kindly, 'I am sorry Olivia, but I am tired and need to go back to home.' and then walked away straight out the hall. This broke Olivia's heart and she kept looking at him again till he had disappeared.

CHAPTER 5
UNEXPECTED ENCOUNTER

The next day in the office went with the silent treatment from Olivia. David was too much into his own work that he didn't even notice Olivia's anger and that frustrated her even more.

'What *is* it with him?' questioned Olivia while she was staring in contempt towards David. He was busy working in his glass cabin and was much focused on this deal of Mr Collins that they had acquired. Matthew was so happy with the performance of David and others hated that somewhere.

'I had warned you...he doesn't allow anyone to come close to him.' spoke Sarah.

'It's frustrating.' spoke Olivia in contempt.

'Because he is desirable and contemptible at the same time.' spoke Sarah.

'Yeah.' Olivia hatefully admitted.

'Been there.' said Sarah and laughed. 'Oh girl, you better allow someone else to break your heart. That boy is done with people.'

The hard work in the office was finally over and David felt happy that the progress him and his team was making was rather commendable. The work satisfaction is what he was trying to have and used his pain as his rage in office. The thought of going back to home haunted him, that means he would be haunted by the memories of Jane and he was scared of that most. It made him feel weak and hopeless no matter what he did all day. All success and all the achievements seemed so little before those torturing emotions.

David climbed down the city bus, after his long day at work, to his regular stop and went to a nearby grocery shop. He took the essentials from there and was heading towards his abode. As he was leaving the grocery store, there was a girl in her mid-twenties calling his name from the other side of the road but David was already, as usual, preoccupied with his thought and could not listen to her. The girl felt disappointed and thought maybe it wouldn't matter as Signior David must have forgotten his waitress of that Italian restaurant: Vanessa. She headed back to her restaurant over her bicycle.

He reached back to his dull, soulless house and then kept himself occupied with cooking some dinner. He grabbed his plate and went to his room and opened up YouTube to watch something on it. He had no attention to what he was eating. He just knew that it was his time to have dinner and the body needed some food to function but the heart, it was lingering somewhere else.

Haunted by all the memories and internal pain, David had a tough night and had difficulty falling asleep. Better half, he thought and then thought it is better to be whole in oneself. Why need someone else to feel content in life? Why keep changing ourselves constantly so that we can be agreeable and acceptable to the people? Will there be at least one person who shall accept us for what we are?

After a time he was sick of these thoughts and knew that it had no point in today's world. One must keep the upper lip about these needs and endure them in private or better to not feel them at all. But how? Ultimately when our day ends and we may achieve many goals but yet...yet when we go to sleep, a thought before falling asleep is that 'After all, I just want to be loved.'

Basics have become rare these days and unnecessary things have become needs. Walking alone in full of people with different thoughts while you are trying to sustain the faith in your heart that someday...someday you shall find what you were looking for, is one of the hardest battles some face. All are going through the same thing but yet nobody is taking a risk to open up about it. And why should one? When people tried to open up they ended up getting judged.

It's uncanny how many suffered the same issue but still failed to empathize with another. Zeus had indeed separated humans, thought David, it's a tragedy that many were failing to find the one person whom they could truly feel connected. He thought of how he had felt connected with Jane and yet ultimately where it led and then thought it's all just foolish to engage in such thoughts. Maybe there is no point in anything at all, not even in these sufferings, he thought and with such thoughts, he got tired and fell asleep.

Few days passed in work until the weekend had arrived. It was a Saturday morning and David was in a Red-roaster Coffee shop having his Cod and Egg Yolk Rosti. The weather was lively today. Sun was out and people were relishing the warm weather. David felt good today and was having his meal while checking up the updates and news of the market on his phone. He couldn't eat anything without watching something over his phone, a very bad habit he had recently adopted. Perhaps eating quietly had made him feel lonelier.

After a while, David casually looked out of the windshield of the shop and saw a girl on a bicycle was passing by. The sky-blue bicycle and basket on the front had suddenly reassured him that it was indeed the one he was thinking about: Vanessa. He promptly stood up and headed towards the door but the customer in the shop had become obstruction over his way and till he got out the shop, Vanessa was long gone. David could still see her but there was no point calling her name. He had felt strange that he did feel an urge to come out and to say hello to her. Somewhere David regretted not taking Vanessa's phone number. He could have just simply called her and asked to meet. Perhaps, now he did feel like meeting her again but he wasn't sure if she shall remember him or if she would even want to talk to him.

[Sunday Morning]

Next morning David was taking the same route, St James's St. to run as he had taken last Sunday, in a hope that once again he shall come across Vanessa. As he was crossing by the intersection where they both were to collide last time, he waited for a while to see if she was coming from that same route, but she didn't. Maybe she doesn't always come at this time, thought David. He even thought of trying to go to the restaurant again but then feared that Vanessa might think that he's stalking her. He lingered on that route for a while but there was no sign of Vanessa that morning and he felt a bit off and returned to his home disappointed.

After returning home he took a bath and got dressed, looking like the classy Brit-bachelor. Running had exhausted him a lot and he was out to have a coffee and breakfast at a shop called My Coffee Story on the same St James's St. David had a book along with him. The 2400 years old content he held, The Symposium by Plato.

He ordered the coffee and some sandwiches along with it. While the order had still time to come up over his table, he opened up the book and started to read. Whenever he was tormented by life, David would find solace in books. They would guide him and help him to deal with life's challenges. Talking with someone was perhaps wasn't an option for him as most people lacked to empathize with his sufferings so he would always retreat to books over weekends. The only time where he could read peacefully. He had satisfaction over the progress he had made over this week in his deal with Mr Collins. Matthew was happy and they had another meeting with Mr Collins tomorrow for which David was excited. He was leading the team, after all.

As the order had reached over his table, he exchanged a polite nod with a waitress and finally put the book aside. He had finished 15 pages of the book within that period. After the long run, he was starving and now grabbed the sandwiches first and took a sip of black coffee to wash it down. David's all attention was into this breakfast that he didn't notice that a girl in a black pencil bottom jeans and white top wearing a coral color sweater above it, with a little sack over her shoulder, had entered the coffee shop. And she had grabbed the corner table, where there was a window on one side. She took out a book and put it over the table. She called for a waiter and ordered Espresso and soon was her attention all in the book.

David had finished his sandwiches and took a last sip of his black coffee. As he was putting down the cup his eyes fell over this pretty girl who was lost into reading a book and had tense expressions over her face. He kept looking at her for a moment, maybe the reading part was difficult to read, judging by her expressions he thought. But David was pleased that finally he had received his opportunity to meet the person who he wanted to for days: Vanessa.

He grabbed the tissue papers and wiped his hands and his mouth. He checked his appearance over the front camera of his mobile phone. Assured of his proper appearance he stood up grabbing his own book and walked slowly and hesitantly towards Vanessa. She was still drowned into her book that she didn't even look at him and said,

'Put the Espresso on the table. Thank you.' and she kept reading. She mistook him for a waiter and he smiled looking at her. Maybe he liked how she was too much into the book that she didn't care about her surroundings. A short moment passed until the waiter came up with her order and she got a bit disturbed and finally looked up from her book.

She first looked at the waiter as he was going then her eyes fell over a tall young man who was standing before her. Vanessa felt that her breath got stuck into her chest as she saw Signor David standing before her, smiling, looking pleased to see her.

'Hi Vanessa.' said David and gave a very pleasant smile.

She was still in a little shock from this unexpected encounter she had with David was still taking time to process it. She was still and looking at him iced.

'It's been a long time. How are you?' Those words felt so warm to her in that chill moment of soft thrill she experienced. Seeing her steady stare at him, had made him feel that maybe she hadn't recognized him. He was feeling awkward for his move now, 'Um...David?' he said, trying to remind her of him. 'Signor David, perhaps?'

Vanessa pressed her lips hard to suppress her amusement which had derived from David's effort to remind her of who he was. She got up and spoke, 'I remember you...David.' said Vanessa. She remembered how he had asked her to not call him Signor outside of her restaurant. He felt better to hear that. 'I was just taken aback to see you here. It was....'

'Unexpected.' completed David.

'Yeah...unexpected.' she seemed pleased to see him too. For a moment they both were silent and were thinking what to speak.

'Um...what are you reading?' asked David after seeing the book she had clutched so hard in her right hand. Perhaps she was nervous. She turned up the book and showed the cover page.

'Wuthering Heights.' said David. He knew this painful book. No doubt the expressions over Vanessa's face were tensed. He remembered he had asked someone to buy it and store it in the book collection.

'It's a very difficult book...to read.' confessed Vanessa.

'I know I have read it. It's one of my favorites.' admitted David.

'You like reading?' asked her.

He smiled and showed her the book he had in his own hand. She looked at it and smiled and looked back straight to him.

'Well...' they both said at same time. Something there was that they both needed to tell.

'After you.' spoke David gently.

'No after you.' she said a bit childishly. She was curious to know what he had to say.

David smiled and was a bit shy and hesitant while speaking, 'Well...I was just...um...feeling like to...'

'Yes.' she asked curiously, looking straight into his eyes.

He looked in her eyes and felt a bit lost. The time had paused for a moment and the phone rang which broke the trance.

It was Vanessa's father. She picked up the call, 'Si padre?'

David couldn't understand what that meant but he stood there waiting.

'Saro li presto.' she answered and put down the phone and looked back to David. 'I'm sorry.' she felt guilty. 'I'll have to go...something came up. I am needed at...'

'I understand.' spoke David in a low tone. He did feel a little pang that maybe it won't happen. He felt a strong need to talk with her and now when he had gotten a chance; it was being taken away from him.

'Yeah...' he tried to suppress his pang.

Vanessa grabbed her bag and put the book in it and left money around her untouched Espresso. She seemed in a hurry. He quietly took a step aside to let her pass. This annoyed her somewhere that she had to leave just like that. She didn't like it either but she had to go.

David didn't muster the courage to say to her something. He just let her go like this is what always happens to him. There was some pain in his eyes which he hid looking down all this time.

'Do you often come to this coffee shop?' asked Vanessa after turning around a step ahead of him.

'Uh...no...I came here today randomly.' confessed David. The short pause lingered and he asked her return, 'You?' Maybe he hoped that if she comes here regularly then there are pretty good chances to walk into each other.

'Sometimes....once in two weeks perhaps...especially when I want to read.' said her.

'Oh.' so there was a low probability of them meeting again. Unless he goes to her restaurant but he was nervous that he might cast an impression of a stalker and also that he cared enough to see her, which was quite contrary to his reputation.

Vanessa was reading all the things over his face. Her deep eyes pierced the shield he had put and looked straight into him, which at the same time made him uncomfortable and comfortable. 'But I'll be going to the pier this evening.' said her. 'To spend some ME time.' For a moment he couldn't understand what she meant. 'Maybe then you can tell me more about Jane.' and he got her hint.

He smiled and nodded. She smiled back at him, 'Bye David.'

'Bye Vanessa.' he said and watched her going out of the coffee shop until she went out of his sight. He still felt her presence there as her Autumn perfume lingered for a while after she had gone.

It was getting difficult for him to be patient and now all he was waiting for was sundown.

[Evening]

David got ready and was excited about going on the pier and running into Vanessa. Along his walk to pier his feet stopped at a flower shop. He thought of getting white lilies for Vanessa but then he thought it might look too much for the beginning of this new friendship and might cast a wrong impression. So he dropped the idea and walked ahead empty handed. The thought of buying a car was finally running into his head and somewhere he was beginning to feel regret for not buying one yet. With all the thoughts of little and big regrets along with the excitement to see Vanessa again, he could not notice how the time had passed when he had reached Brighton Beach. He stopped there looking at Pier. Today Sun was out and it had cast a golden effect on Pier giving it an impression of Mount Olympus.

David looked at Pier hopefully for a while. He was truly hoping that this should not turn out to be his another disappointment. After making up his mind he headed for Pier and after looking for half an hour David had finally found Vanessa, standing alone at the edge, enjoying the sunset. He looked at her for a moment. It reminded him of himself, that there was a feeling of longing on her face, similar to David's. He walked slowly to her, stopping a little distance behind her.

'Just to be safe. You do not come from a mafia family, do you?' asked David to Vanessa.

Recognizing David's voice she turned around smiling gladly, saying, 'Why because I'm an Italian?'

'Well, I've seen The Godfather.' David joked.

Vanessa laughed, '*Italians have a little joke, that the world is so hard a man must have two fathers to look after him, and that's why they have godfathers.*' quoting The Godfather. David was quiet over that quote and he thought about someone, someone who was important and close to him.

He smiled and walked up-to the Vanessa. 'Looking at the sun set, alone. Are you thinking about something?'

Vanessa took a moment to respond, 'Just some internal battle. I take a day off to spend it with myself. I feel distant from myself when I have to spend most of the time among people. I learnt the value of spending time with myself after my prior faith was broken that the value to my life comes from my partner and not from my own.' David was quiet. He understood that it was Vanessa's moment to let her lighten her own burden after they had a talk last Sunday about him. 'How frustrating it is that you finally get something to believe on in your life, after nothing made sense, you think that this thing will give meaning to your life, to your existence and you completely devote yourself to it and then all the hopes and dreams are collapsed just like that when the next person withdraws himself from your life. Everything you built starts to fall down along with your faith in life. And now you don't want to attach again to someone. You are scared to take that risk.'

While David had his eyes on Vanessa, she was speaking out her heart looking at the drowning sun, like it was representing the drowning hope.

David joined her and he also looked at the sun. 'I don't understand myself, what am I stuck to? I'm stuck on her or the kind of memories I had with her? Acceptance is quite difficult, quite painful. We have to accept that we are not that important that we once were.'

Vanessa felt related with David's words. She became so curious to know about David's story.

'Tell me about Jane.' she said, still staring at the sun set.

David paused for a couple of moments. 'Jane was not just my girlfriend.' he said quite serenely. 'We were best-friends first.' Vanessa looked at him, she was somewhere surprised. 'We were quite inseparable. We both lived in the same neighborhood. I was 20 when we first met and she was 16. We both were loved and approved at each other's home and we often spent time at home, talking about things, studying together, planning business achievements and then watching lots of movies together. Eat together and even cook together sometimes. We both used to be there for each other in time of needs and things like time and distance never mattered in our friendship. It was all so good and perfect. I had found an honest friend for myself and I had alienated my old phony friends. It was her friendship, a promise to be my friend, that had given me courage to leave the toxic friendships. I had worse fear of falling alone than being into a toxic friendship.'

'She chose what was good for you.' said Vanessa.

'It was reciprocal in almost everything and I never felt compatible with anyone else like that. I was also looking, my future, in someone else. Just like you. Then after two years of friendship, we both fell in love slowly and then all of it at once. And being in a relationship with her felt nothing different. We still acted with each other as we did in our friendships, except kisses and intimate hugs. You know in those moments I truly lived my life. I was truly happy and I miss that.' said David miserably.

'Then what changed when things were so fine between you two?' wondered Vanessa.

'Situations, I think, change every relation eventually.' answered David. 'I played a huge part in convincing her mother to allow her to go to London for further studies. Her mother wasn't ready as she was a single mother. Jane's father had died in a car accident when she was 14.'

'That's terrible!' exclaimed Vanessa.

'I was treated as part of her family. Her mother loved me like her own son and she was happy to realize later on about our relationship. She supported it instantly. I was not much close with my own parents but they were happy for me. My father liked Jane as his own daughter. That caused me to heal my relations with him because Jane would feel a father's love from him. It was going perfect and I was so...so hopeful. But then suddenly everything changed, the things that were holding us together, our trust in each other, was broken. And it broke my whole world that I was building. It turned out that she fell for another friend from London and she cheated on me. And when I found out, she said that I wasn't there for her. She didn't know what she was doing. And she was giving all those reasons people generally give once they commit infidelity.' Tears had filled up David's eyes but he just let them flow. 'I was so much into her that I begged her to come back and I'll accept her after everything else but, she was so infatuated with that new guy that all this six years of friendship failed so easily that it meant nothing in the end for her.' David's heart was filled and he sighed, controlling so hard to hold his cry. Vanessa felt like putting her hand over his shoulder but David was so serene and so miserable that she thought it's better to let it all come out as it is. Let him process his own pain with his own pace and capacity.

'She had given me headphones on my birthday. They meant so special to me that I didn't let them touch anyone, thinking that they would be contaminated.' He laughed to himself. 'But when the person is touched by someone else by her own will, then it contaminates the LOVE and it makes things really difficult to accept. I was feeling so stupid that while I was not allowing anyone else to touch the gifts she had given to me, she allowed herself into someone else's bed.'

Vanessa was speechless, she thought she could empathize with David but his pain was beyond her capacities.

'I felt so repulsed from the core of my soul for all the emotions I had stored for her. All my dreams, MY HOME that I had found in her was all broken so bad. I just kept asking WHY? And there was no answer. What was my fault? That I could not see her in London? I thought she understood my situation and I had hidden nothing from her. She was aware of my family's financial condition. There she used to call me that she's missing me so badly and was demanding me to come and see her. She was not wrong to expect that... but when I see my parents having a really tough time to support my educational needs... then I just can't have that time with her. How could I? In the process of being a good boyfriend I was becoming a bad son.' A huge guilt was seen in David's words and Vanessa was just idle and all focused on him. 'I agree that I didn't get along with my parents much but I was still their son and they were my parents and I loved them.'

David wiped his eyes with his bare hands and sniffed.

'It is the sight that kills a person most to see that his ex-partner, who promised worlds with him/her, is now, how easily, making new promises with a new person in their lives. And we are still stuck into the old promises with them.' David paused for a while. He sighed and spoke, 'Later on to realize that they were taking pleasure in torturing us with that sight, them being with someone else hurts us and they know it. And they kill us everyday with that thought, just a little every fucking day.'

'It is often the honest one stays alone after being cheated on but I just don't understand when she didn't just cheated you, she literally annihilated you, then why are you still alone? Why didn't you get with someone else? I know it's difficult to be with someone else after such experience but still what stopped you?'

'The idea that then there would be no difference between I and her.' said David. 'Best revenge is to not be like the person who caused you a hurt.'

Vanessa looked at him adoringly.

'I learnt that lesson from Marcus Aurelius.' professed David, 'But I admit that it hurts really bad knowing that it's not ME. It's someone else in her life now. Eyes saw these things but the heart still can't accept it. I feel so ashamed to have felt all these emotions for her in the first place.'

‘You didn't know at that time that it would turn out like this.' said Vanessa.

‘No I didn't but I should have.'

‘You couldn't have.' said Vanessa, ‘David it is the responsibility of the next person to sustain our faith. Situations are always gonna change but bonding must remain immune to changing circumstances.'

‘But it didn't, did it? They break it with their own hands, leaving us with a shame of loving them at the first place. Suddenly you become wrong in your own eyes for the betrayal committed by the other person.'

Vanessa felt so angry and frustrated, ‘What a bitch!'

David got angry, ‘Don't call her that.'

Vanessa was taken aback. She could not understand him at all. He cared for her even after everything that happened to him?

‘You won't tell anyone about her because you don't want anyone else to think bad of her, do you?' spoke Vanessa. ‘Even after getting cheated, it still hurts you if someone speaks ill of her? Ohhh David, why? After all, why did you love her so much?

'Because I saw a life in her which I never got to live.'

Vanessa was looking at him puzzled and yet admiring at the same time. She realized that she liked David and it was annoying her, his unconditional love for Jane. She did feel contempt for Jane in her heart for treating David like this.

'David, it's not living. You can't live your life into past good memories.'

'Moving on doesn't mean you get over the person who cheated on you by being with someone else to forget them.' answered David.

'No but it's learning to live without them and be truly happy with yourself.' said Vanessa with a striking authority in her eyes and voice.

She was looking in his eyes and for a while David's eyes lingered in her eyes. He felt connected and so did her. She took a step ahead slowly and came close to David. She could feel the warmth of his body and the smell of his cologne. She came closer and her lips were inches apart from David's. Time was paused for a while Vanessa had closed her eyes and David did feel the temptation of her touch. He tried to get close too and when their lips were barely an inch apart Jane's face came to David's head and stood before his eyes. He recoiled a little. Vanessa sensed that and opened her eyes then he recoiled all of him. She took a step behind from him as well.

She felt so bad and hurt, 'What happened David? You still felt like cheating on her memories?'

David was speechless and he couldn't speak a word to her and then suddenly in that silent moment the bell of his phone rang so loud. He couldn't understand for a few seconds that his phone was ringing then he pulled out his cell phone and went to the edge, a few steps away from Vanessa.

'This is David.' he said in his grave voice as he picked up the call. And then a voice spoke to him something that threw a thunderbolt on his expressions. His face turned into panic and tense mode. Vanessa noticed that something was wrong. David was silent and he put the phone down.

'What happened David?' asked Vanessa.

David looked at her...

CHAPTER 6
SEVERANCE FROM HAPPINESS

'I've mailed him everything already,' said David on the phone. 'I am sorry that I had to leave suddenly like this.

'David, you've been a faithful employee. Your dedication was always admirable, so don't feel burdened.' answered Matthew, boss of David in RockLand Corporation.

'It's just we worked a lot for this deal today and I feel guilty that I couldn't be there in such imperative times.' David said apologetically.

'David, there are other responsibilities too in life than the job. You are where you should be right now. How is he?' asked Matthew concernedly.

'Doctor says his condition is critical and does not have much time.' David answered numbly.

'Oh! I am sorry to hear that. You take as much time as you need.'

'Thanks Matthew.' and he put the phone down.

David was in the foyer of Royal Edinburgh Hospital. He stood there mulling over these sad thoughts for a moment and then returned to the hospital room.

There was Agatha sitting on the chair and a man in his late fifties lying on the hospital bed, sedated. The ambience was difficult for David. His father was drawing his last breath on a hospital bed, blessing of the habit of excessive drinking and smoking. And there was his mother with whom he had not talked or seen for the last two years after the hurtful events of his life. He couldn't bear her presence but the situation had put a lock on his mouth.

'I knew you'd come back.' said Agatha after several minutes of silence.

David scoffed, feeling repulsed.

'I understand that you wouldn't want to see me but in times like this David...'

David stared at her angrily and an outburst of his emotional frustration came out, 'Time like this? As if you have always cared for difficult times, mother.'

'I am sorry David for leaving both of you like that.'

'Oh just save it! You always hated him. You always thought that you married a man who is a lot beneath you. And now you are coming here showing your fake care. At least be brave enough to show your true stand.'

'David it was mutually decided. I and Jefferson both had agreed to a separation.' Agatha justified.

'His accord came from knowing the fact that *he* failed in holding you after you said those hurtful words.' said David. 'You were not happy, that's what you had said. Happy. Mother, your definition of happiness comes from materialistic comforts only. Ever cared how it affected me when I spent my whole childhood seeing both parents fighting all the time and feeling ignored constantly.'
Agatha felt shameful and remorseful. 'David we both were just fighting and we wanted to get separate early but then Jefferson asked me to not until you finish your education.' David looked at his dying father. 'You had continued your education because of that girl. And then even I thought that I should put up till you are capable of taking responsibility for your own life.'

'Oh so I should take it as an act of care?' David grunted with anger. 'I was a college drop out because I was sick of everything, because of you...both of you.' David said hatefully. 'I tried to speak to you about my problems mom but you didn't care. I stopped coming at you. I stopped expecting anything.'

'I'm sorry David.' said Agatha.

'It doesn't matter now mother. The damage is done. Life has always been unfair, it gives you things that you never expected and makes you happy then take it all back in an instant leaving you confused and damaged.'

'You've changed a lot.' acknowledged Agatha.

'Hard times mould people into unknown.' said David looking at his lying sick father. 'Once he is gone, you shall never see me again. We shall have no contacts.'

'David please.'

'A woman, who left the family in times of crises, is no longer my concern. I am sufficiently capable to handle my life and I seek no support from things like family. I realized one thing when you left mother...' he looked disdainfully at her.

'What?' she asked.

'Families do not stay together out of emotional bonding but the financial dependence.'

Agatha felt ashamed. She was sick of the poverty and she had left the family with the first chance she got to separate, in the name of seeking her individuality.

'I feel shame that I used to believe in things like family even though I didn't have one, even when both my parents lived.' He said painfully, 'Not everyone gets to spend time with their parents mother.' David thought of Jane and her deprivation of her father. 'If I didn't have thought about problems at home and would have been a little selfish, then perhaps my life would have been different right now.' and then he got out of the room.

[At Hospital Canteen]

David had been there all day and didn't have a meal. All the gloomy thoughts and vibes had consumed him enough that he didn't even feel like eating something. It's such a curious thing, whenever our heart is stern it is our stomach that pays the price for it first. When he finally felt like eating something, after tired of the same negative thoughts running over his head, he went to the hospital canteen where families of patients could have a meal while they waited there all day. After having three sandwiches he came back to counter again.

'One coffee please.' David asked at the canteen counter.

'Make it two.' A woman's voice came from behind. David looked back. He knew that voice and yet he was surprised a bit to hear it there. He didn't say a word and got two coffees from the counter and headed quietly to the vacant table at the corner of the canteen. The woman followed him and joined him on the table.

'Hello David, long time.' the woman started the conversation. 'It's good to see you.'

David was quiet and looked a bit frustrated and annoyed but was putting lots of efforts to keep his composure.

'What are you doing here Pam?' David spoke off.

To that, Pamela felt very strange and unwelcome. She did feel a little bad but then she thought that she should have expected that.

'I heard the news.' answered Pamela. 'I came to the hospital as soon as I could.' She said while appearing concerned about David and his family.

'I didn't expect you here, after all that happened.' answered David.

'David I am friends with your family too.' answered Pamela.

'That's because I and Jane wanted you to be and it should have been over as I and Jane got separated.' said David coldly, denying the validation of her claim.

Pamela was quiet for a moment and thought to arrange her words more carefully but she couldn't understand how. She had concerns which she needed to speak out to him.

'Is it too easy for you people to break things off?' David was quietly having his coffee.

'Pam we had talked about this two years ago I don't see any point repeating it.' David answered indifferently.

'Are you telling me that you have finally learnt to move on in life?' asked Pamela.

David was quiet and stared at her. Then after a while he asked directly, 'What are you trying to pull off Pamela?'

'You know what I always wanted.' answered Pamela.

'That's not going to happen.' confirmed David.

'You young people these days give up on a relationship too soon. What do you expect a relationship to be? A constant source of pleasure and happy time? It consists of both good and bad times David. I thought you understood that well.'

'You think I did not understand that?' David had lost his cool and for the first time he got angry on Pamela. 'Or is it you who wants to make up for Jane's sins?' Pamela was quiet after those words.

'Tell me, does that diminish my value too in your life after what Jane did to you?' demanded Pamela.

'You should have asked that to Jane, Pam. It was her demand that I keep no contacts with you. You should have educated her about relationships as you are trying to do with me.'

'You think I didn't make efforts to convince her?' Pamela said it like she was deeply wounded by those words.

'You knew that as well as I knew how stubborn she always was. Whatever was decided, it was right in front of you.' David said.

'I know.' confirmed Pamela with a full of remorse in her voice.

'Then I don't understand why you are trying to change things again? It wouldn't go back to the things as they were before or is it just you Pam who can't take it?'

'You DO know that I couldn't take it at that time too.' Pamela was too sentimental speaking those words out. 'I knew it was all wrong.'

'And now you are trying to make it right by trying to bring both Jane and I together? Hmm. Charming.' David said nagging Pam disclosing his anger.

'I would take all the efforts to do that even without any ray of hope.' answered Pam with full determination.

'Pam it wasn't your fault. You don't have to feel guilt for the actions of Jane. And besides Jefferson is taking his last breath on the hospital bed and now is not the time to talk about these things.'

'I have concerns that need to be spoken and David I understand now, it might look like a wrong time but trust me it is the right time because after Jefferson is gone, you will have no reason to come back here.'

'That's quite right Pamela Abernathy and I request you to not pull me back to the things that it took me lots of efforts to get out.' pleaded David.

Pamela was silent for a moment and had a sip of coffee, 'Is that why you are still alone David because you got out of it? You could have been with anyone else. It was her who made the mistake and there was nothing that was holding you back, and yet you chose to be alone. Why?' wondered Pamela.

'Pam please.' said David begging.

'Because you never got out of it. You did love her truly, didn't you? And that's why you don't want to have with someone else what you had with her. You remember you had said that to me before going?' Pamela tried to remind David his last words he spoke to her before going away from everyone. 'This is rare in today's world I must admit and yes I don't want Jane to make such a grave mistake of losing you. Losing a love that is rare but genuine.'

'She has lost me.' David answered.

'Did she?' Pamela doubted implying a hope in David, 'I doubt that....tell me David don't you miss her? In order to feel happy inside, don't you miss Jane Abernathy?'

David was serene and it felt like Pam had just reopened a closed wound. 'Going back to her memories to feel happy is like drinking poison to quench the thirst. It makes me feel so good but it ends with pain. I did tell you at that time Pam that I shall miss Jane but I will still not want her back in my life.'

'I'm not trying it all because she's my daughter.' she paused and took a sniffing breath. 'I care for you too David.' Pamela said with huge concern in her heart. 'And I need you to drop your ego and see what your heart needs.'

'My EGO?' David's outburst was violent. 'It was Jane who cheated me. It was her who broke the trust and you are questioning my ego?'

'I'm sorry David... I didn't mean it like that. It's...' Pamela was trying to control the damage of her words.

'Do you even know HOW IT FEELS?' David had tears in his eyes. Pam was silently looking in his eyes, all that hurt and that helplessness was unbearable to her. 'Whenever I think of Jane with that guy, and being with him as she was with me.... it... it disgusts my soul from the core. It boils my blood even to think of Jane with that guy.'

'I am sorry David. I...'

'It's so-so fucking frustrating Pam. I am really trying hard to hold it and act. Alright? Let me.'

'Okay. I'm sorry that I upset you. But David can't you see it is hurting you too. All I am asking you to deal with it...I know you are hurt and I know you still miss her because you love her.'

David recoiled and wiped his tears. He was hurting and all the efforts to hold it all inside were failing.

'After two years I still can't believe that she can do this to me. I loved her. I loved that girl so much and she broke it all off. It's not my ego Pam that holds me back from going back to her, it's my incapability to trust her again that truly holds me back. I can't trust her. She is not what she used to be. She shall realize her mistake but then that would be too late...'

'It's not too late David.'

'Pam she is an angel in my memories and I'd keep her like that and I do not wish to lose that feeling when I bring reality into it. She is good in my memories and let her be.'

'Why won't you take a chance of bringing her back to your life then?' asked Pamela. 'I was always living in a hope for this one day and it has come.'

'What do you mean?' said David.

'Jane has left London and has come back to Edinburgh since last few months. I was not aware of it first but she had gone to Limerick for a few weeks and then returned here.'

'Limerick?' exclaimed David. 'I didn't think she would ever go back there.' Limerick was Jane's father's birthplace, where she had spent early years of her childhood and had often talked about it with David when they both were new in friendship. David would just love to hear her stories of Limerick with her father. He had never seen Jane happier when she talked about Limerick because that's where she had the most beautiful memories with her father. After talking about her father she would start crying and then David would hold her and Jane would cry to her heart. She never felt comfortable crying like she did when she hugged him.

David was put into the old memories which softened his rude and unwelcome behaviour towards Pamela. And then slowly his eyes were filled with tears. He was missing what he had. He was missing it so hard.

'I hated you, Pam.' He pointed his finger at her. 'I hated you for not saving things.' David sniffed, fighting his tears. God damn it. I had everything, Pam. I didn't just love Jane. I loved everything else around her, even you. You were my family and you failed to convince her.'

'Then why did you go away even from me David?'

'You know it was Jane who asked that from me. She wasn't okay that I kept contact with her family after things got broken so don't you blame me for breaking relations so easily.' explained David.

'I know but still, why did YOU go away.' David looked at Pam. She was so hurtful and it was clear that she missed him so much and she was empathizing to the point that, was it really had to be this way? He could have been defiant to Jane but he chose not to.

'Because then I'd have spoken up to you of my sufferings like you are my family. It felt so weak to talk to you about it. I felt so ashamed that after everything I am keeping contact with you. It was indecorous. So in order to refrain myself from getting into more attachment, I distanced myself from you, saving my dignity.'

'Do you even know how I lived all these years in that home?' said Pamela. 'I used to feel support because of you and I would not worry about things because then there would be you handling the coming troubles. You were like my son to me and I even formed that reading habit in me. I read all those books which you insisted on buying. That home wasn't what it used to be after you had gone.'

'I don't feel those emotions anymore Pam. I no longer feel that I am your son. I did feel once and I felt so proud but then I must maintain the proprieties. I can't be your son even if I want to. Even if I loved being one at some point of my life. But now... everything is changed. Everything after how she treated me that night, right before your eyes when you tried to patch us together. But she insulted me. She humiliated me that I am not man enough to take the damage to myself and open up to you, her mother. How can I forget such humiliation Pam? After that even Agatha got separated from Jefferson. I was going through hell and yet I called her and asked her to don't leave me alone in such a difficult time... but do you even know what she said to me?'

Pam looked down in shame. She knew how her sweet daughter had treated him.

'Those are your problems David, what do you expect from me? I don't care anymore about it.' completed David and looked at Pam with a hateful stare. 'I hated her because she separated me even from you. She took pleasure in that, knowing that it will indeed hurt me badly and it did. Both of my parents were alive but I never got that affection from them what one gets from his parents... but that I got from you, Pamela. And she severed me from such happiness in my life. She humiliated me for expecting motherly affection from her own mother, you. I felt so so stupid to get attached to people and think that they will also involve me into their family.' David still felt ashamed for developing such emotions in his heart. How could he stop himself? He believed that home is where he is happy and he was happy with Jane and Pam.

Pam always supported and stood for David. He had everything but had to lose it for the sake of the proprieties.

'I can't even spell out my actual suffering even if I compare all the hellish things there are to describe my hurt. It still won't be equivalent to the actual suffering that I am going through.' said David.

'Why did you not at least call me then? Talk out your heart and feel better about it. Why did you hold it inside and let it turn into poison?'

'Pride won't allow me emotional comforts, Pam. If I come and talk to you about my suffering that wouldn't have looked like I am seeking comfort from my family member in harsh times but as a weak boy who could not handle his heartbreak, just like Jane had said it.' answered David.

'You are not a weak person David. Feeling hurt is only natural. You've got hurt, that means you were attached in the first place.'

'But did she care to see in that perspective?' asked David, 'I grew up in the darkness of loneliness, when Jane came to my life I had a semblance of hope that I'll never live like this anymore but she only put me deep into that darkness. I can't come and talk to you Pam, no matter how much I long for it in my lonely moments. You will still be her mother and I just can't come up and talk about my problems to you.'

'You know that I am always there for you. If you need help I am there. Just come back home.'

'I know you stood behind me in all the circumstances like a family does. And I really admire you for that, being with someone else makes me feel like I am cheating on my memories with Jane.' David thought about Vanessa. 'But I guess soon I'll be over that curse too. I just don't understand why you are so persistent about bringing me back with Jane?'

Pamela fell silent. She took her time to respond, 'I've seen many colleagues and friends getting married in a whim or in direction of their ego led them, ended up with the biggest regret of their lives. I believe that most relationships fail because people give up on them too soon. And that's what I am afraid of about you two.'

David just maintained his stare at Pamela.

'I still have those gifts which you returned. Jane wanted to get rid of them but I preserved it, thinking that right now you both are not in the right mind and shall regret later in future.' said Pamela. 'Do you still feel repulsively angry at Jane that she allowed herself to be... touched?'

'How do you imagine that I can get over that thing?' asked David.

'Just come back home, please. You have a good heart, David.'

'That doesn't mean you can ask me to go back to her.' he answered.

'Have you lost that too? Your good heart?' asked Pamela.

'A good person loses everything in the end Pam, even their good intentions. I won't hide from you that I don't miss her, I do but I have no intention to bring her back in my life.' David stated as final decision and stood up to leave.

'She still loves you, David.' Pam said, staring at her half-empty coffee cup. David was frozen to his place and then turned around and looked at Pam curiously. Pam looked at him. 'Jane still loves you. She is at home right now and I see her lost in guilt and I cannot bear the sight of her being like that.' Pamela's eyes were filling up with fresh tears. 'As I had told you two years ago that I can't force her to stop and be with you, the same way today I can't force you to stop and be with her; even if I really want to.' Pamela stood up and walked up to David. 'Look after Jefferson. Spend your time with him and try to make it count.' David looked down in little shame. Pam hugged him and said. 'Home is where you are happy.'

CHAPTER 7
FORGIVE YOURSELF

After returning from the canteen, in the hospital room, David was looking at Agatha. She was trying to avoid his direct eye contact and was looking nervous a bit.

'It was you who told Pamela that I was probably in the hospital canteen, right?' asked David interrogatively.

I don't know what you are talking about.' Agatha replied.

'I am asking, are you making some sort of efforts to redress issues of my life?' asked David.

'NO.' answered Agatha.

'Good, because I must tell you that nothing can make things better between us. And I'd appreciate that until I am here that you don't try to control issues in my life.'

'David, I know you hate me and there is a very good reason for that too but I am not prying into your life. Pamela came here to see Jefferson and then inquired about you too. I just replied that yes you have come and then it was her who wanted to see you. I didn't try to cajole her, alright?'

David was quiet. He felt wounded to lose an argument with his mother. In a more accurate sense he felt frustrated that Pamela had actually cared for him and he couldn't accept it because it was opposite to his prior beliefs. The stare between both Agatha and David stayed for a few moments until they both were distracted by a pleasant intervention.

'I thought I was the only one who fought with you.' said Jefferson had come to consciousness moments ago but was witnessing quietly the little family drama.

'Jeff.' Agatha exclaimed in pleasure and came to him. 'I thought you'd never come back to your senses.'

'I have a habit of disappointing you.' answered Jefferson and laughed a little. Agatha made a face.

'Wow. You guys can't even stop fighting even for a second, can you?' asked David disdainfully.

Jefferson looked pleasantly at his son who had come to see him in his last moments. David also looked straight in his eyes. For a moment there was silence and all three of them together for that moment. But Jefferson looked more into David and understanding his limited time he asked...

'I need to talk with David. Leave us the room.' asked Jefferson.

Agatha looked at Jefferson totally taken aback but he didn't break his stare at his son. She then looked at David but he also ignored her and didn't even look at her. Feeling insulted a bit she went out of the hospital room closing the door behind her.

And suddenly the room was so quiet that the beeps of hospital equipment were sounding so loud. Breaking such tormenting silence Jefferson spoke off to David.

'What a sight!' said Jefferson in hoisting his enthusiasm which David often saw after Jeff was getting drunk. 'Two dead people in this damn room.' said coughing lightly.

'Two?' asked David, slightly getting curious about his words. He knew his father well because how he always talked implying things in the next person.

'There are two sorts of death.' said Jefferson in his weak voice. 'One is physical and second is spiritual.'

David closed his eyes and shook his head in annoyance. 'Even on death bed, you can't spare me of your Kierkegaard philosophy?'

'Ugh! Look at you. How miserable you are.' Jefferson said in disgust. 'You should start to drink.'

'Oh yeah? Then be what? Abusive and cowardly like you? No thanks.' answered David.

'I drank in order to live.' Replied Jefferson.

'And look where that brought you.' Nagged David.

'Yeah, and I have no regret for that. I am on this hospital bed and yet it is you who is dead already.'

'What do you mean?'

'Look at you. How miserable and lone. For what?'

'You won't understand that.'

'Oh for god's sake. Boy. You loved that girl Jane and it didn't work out, is that why you left the living?' This direct approach from Jefferson had startled David a bit.

'Father I don't think you should worry about that right now. Take it easy.' suggested David thinking about his father's weak health.

'Look David I know it well that...' Jefferson coughed miserably. '...that I don't have much time, and before I go, I want to have the last emotional satisfaction that I, for once, had a true conversation with my own son.'

'Wow. You understand that real quick... in 28 years. Hmm.' said David nagging.

'That's the beauty of death, David. It stimulates anyone from their apathy and forces them to finish the most important things of life which they had been ignoring when they lived.'

'And you think that talking with me was the one important thing you never did?' David asked sentimentally. Jefferson nodded in desperation. David sighed and paused for a moment and then spoke off, 'Yes I am messed up because of Jane and it's been really tough for me.' He looked at Jefferson in expectation that he would judge him but Jeff was quiet.

David thought that it's better to come directly on the point, 'It is because whatever I believed in turned out to be a lie. And when it has happened all the time and now I don't want to believe in anything anymore.' and then David started to feel really annoyed by the inappropriate topic for the moment. He felt so embarrassed that Jeff is gonna talk to him about his love life. 'Can we just knock it off, please? It's really not necessary.'

'Keep talking.' Jefferson commanded like a strict father.

David felt that little better and he spoke obediently yet with frustration, 'I believed that I'd be safe and protected when I was a kid around my father and I'd be loved immeasurably around mom but all you people did was to fight each other and never cared how it affected me. I lost my faith in things like family until I met Jane. With her I felt like a home which was deprived of me, and that's why I always hated you. But then again that hate wasn't as much as I hated myself. Jane cheated and yeah I couldn't take it. I loved her and thought that she could never do that because she loved me too. So Jefferson yes I am fucking miserable, I didn't get the love I needed. You had your satisfaction, can we stop that now?' David finished in a grunt.

Jefferson was extraordinarily calm to all that. He did feel a few pangs but yet he was under pressure to make the maximum of his limited time, 'Oh that was something serious stuff. And I am sorry that I took your childhood from you...' For a moment David looked at his father in hope for love as he did in his childhood. '...but that doesn't mean you got to waste your youth too. Even I didn't get the love I needed and the only way I could feel that love was when I drank.'

David scoffed.

'Rare people get the love they need; most of us are deprived of it because of time and luck. Circumstances fail to even the most passionate lovers. But you gotta keep going, that's life, David. You don't lose people, people lose you, what you truly lose is yourself. And the trick is to not lose yourself no matter what happens in your life.'

'I don't know what I really want. I'm completely messed up in the past.'

'Then get clarity son, of what you truly want. Only then you can make the right choice for yourself.'

After a moment's pause, David spoke, 'She used to believe in my cause that's what gave me strength. It felt good to have a partner alongside me. Someone who really believed in me.' His voice ended on a disappointing note.

'Then what changed?'

'I don't know. She just changed somehow.' said David, still confused for his own feelings. 'Suddenly, one day she stopped talking with me. I called again and again but she wouldn't talk. So I even asked after negative thoughts haunted me in the meantime that, is there someone else and she acted like I have offended her. I felt so bad and I apologized for doubting her like that but I was so insecure at that time because of her such a sudden changed behaviour. Then she met me in Edinburgh and asked me to see her so that she can just tell that she wants to break up with me. And I was offered no explanation. Just a direct verdict that I was not there for her. I was not seeing her in London... Well, I didn't understand how she could be so persistent about it when she knew that we had such a turbulent time at that period. All the loans on you father and the tension at home and then even after that Mom left us. It only made me feel that women can be held together if a man has a good amount of money in his pocket.'

David sighed in desperation. He sat on the chair next to Jefferson. 'All my prior beliefs changed. Everything that I believed was a lie. After keeping me confused and playing with my heart with false flirtation she finally admitted that she had committed infidelity with one of her friends in London. She said that he was there for her.'

'Wow. I never thought she could turn out to be this way.' Jefferson said in surprise. 'I really liked that girl and always tried to treat her as my own.'

'And that's what frustrates me even more. She lost her father at an early age and to fill up that void I even tried to make things better with you so that she could feel fatherly affection around you. Girls are too sensitive for their fathers.'

'Boys are also sensitive for their fathers David, it's just they can't show it as clearly as girls.' Jefferson looked at David acknowledging that he can see his heart is breaking seeing his father like this, even in this moment David was trying so hard to endure it like a man but pain of loved ones bends even to the strongest men on earth. He closed his misty eyes but tears didn't stop and they rolled over.

'Why are families always broken like this father?' David asked desperately.

Jefferson sighed and he thought, what could he possibly give the answer to that question but his son always had such a miserable time and he was truly needed to do something for him before he goes. 'Maybe because there wasn't sufficient money to stick them all together.' answered Jeff from his own experience. Agatha had left Jefferson because financial problems were a stigma for her and estrangement was the way she thought would be her escape from such stigma.

'Money.' said David. 'I play with these numbers every day and never thought people could be bought with these numbers too.' said David in disbelief.

'Well what can you do when people are cheaper these days?' asked Jefferson.

'Yeah!' David thought of how Jane was so changed because that guy could buy her fancy stuff and he couldn't. All he had was his heart and his dedication, which he had given all of it. 'It's all because she was sent to London. She was nice when she was here.' David missed how she was before going to London. 'Big cities do change people.'

'No David, these big cities don't really change people but reveal them. People often find some sort of freedom when they go away in new cities, far from their home. Like they have freedom now which they lacked before. Nobody to stop them from doing something.'

'Sadly I was the one who convinced her mother to let her go there.' David blamed himself.

'Look David, you only tried to give her the best things in your capacity. You wanted her to have a good life and best of experiences. You weren't wrong at your place.'

'Then why did it happen to me?' David asked frustratingly. 'All I was just trying to give her what I could not have myself due to difficult circumstances. She and I could have it all but now because of her actions even I am suffering. I just don't understand why the hell do I always have to suffer for the mistakes of other people around me?' asked David.

'That is exactly why we are having this talk and that's why you shouldn't feel embarrassed to talk to me about it even in my last moments.' said Jefferson. 'David you've always been suffering because of me and Agatha. Your needs were ignored and I suspect the family life you couldn't have with us, you probably had with her. A home, I mean. Where you feel safe, where you can retreat when things are bad, where you...'

'...feel happy.' completed David while a thought of Pamela crossed his head.

'People often say that, 'Don't blame the situation or people.' said Jefferson. 'Primarily because they also heard it in their life by someone else when they were also blaming someone or situation. And now they are transmitting the exact thing to the next person they meet with a similar problem.

But our suffering is sometimes, indeed, caused by someone and how long will we just keep telling ourselves to not feel anything or be neutral? We are wounded by people. We are down because of dark time. We are weakened by situations and yes that's why we are down in life.' Jefferson spoke like a drunk rebellion to social injustice. 'But to outgrow these things the power we need comes from the companionship with our loved ones. We are never stronger alone. It is in fact we are most weak then, we are stronger when we have our loved ones around us.'

'That's the struggling father, the fight in life is against the loved ones to get their affection. What a sad thing!' said David.

Jefferson was tired a bit by all this constant talk and he took some time to rest and then again spoke up, 'Love is reciprocal and one-sided is sweet suffering.' David looked at Jefferson. 'In relationships David if you keep thinking about what the next person wants or likes, you shall be nothing but servile to their pleasure but there wouldn't be love in your own account. The Love you deserve but often not ask for it. Just understand David, your needs also matter and if your partner is not giving any validation to them then it's better that you walk away. Choose the girl who is willing to choose you in your bad circumstances as you will choose one in her bad circumstances. Because cheating is never a mistake David, it was always a choice.' David was quietly taking a lecture from his father. 'They know what will be the consequences of their actions and yet they do it, because at such times they don't want to think about what is at stake but want to succumb to their hidden desires.'

'That's what I am most disgusted with. How could she be with someone else when I still can't because her thoughts will resist me. Because what I believed in will still cause me to not betray that cause myself.' David said annoyingly. 'I'm so stupid. I don't even understand why I am like this?'

'We, men, tend to be romantically in love with one of the miseries of our life. We don't want to let go of that misery. We just hold it and be in it, just to experience it over and over again because we can't get over the feeling, what we once experienced in our lives. We use that misery to define our condition and indulge ourselves into self-pity. Ironic words from a man who drank in self-pity but that's the truth.' Jefferson justified. 'We use that misery to define our condition, and there is a weird pride too in that. People often say it out proudly especially when they are drunk "All that I am today because this one thing had happened then" don't be one of them, David. Don't let an event like these define you. Let them create you and always remember that you can still love again.'

'You speak so many wise things, father. I never knew you could.' David admitted to the wise advice his father was giving him in his limited time.

'Oh! You should have heard me after I got drunk; I could even defeat that son of a bitch Socrates in debate.' and then he laughed a little to himself.

David observed his father how proud he was of his own little achievements. And somewhere David wished that he could only experience such a moment in better situations. After every passing moment, David's will was shattering. He was gonna lose his family member anytime and now was when he was getting that little affection he was seeking from his father and he didn't want it to end.

'David, listen to one thing carefully. When you put up lots of efforts for someone and bring them to the position in life which is a lot better than your own, then it doesn't change them but reveals them and such people will want you again when situations get difficult in their life.'

He thought about it for a few moments. Jane's thoughts were disturbing him a lot at such times. Why so suddenly his own worth was recognized by Jane that Pamela had to come and ask him to come back to her. What if he goes back to her and after things get better then she cheats him again. Once a cheater always a cheater, he thought.

'I was just a medium for her.' David said. 'I looked over her faults. People hide their true version and bring out modesty just because of a difficult time. Once they are out of that time of need, then suddenly modesty falls down and they become rude and ugly.'

'David...' Jefferson said weakly. David looked at him. 'Forgive.'

'I am confused about that.' said David. 'I want to forgive her but when I think about the damages she caused me....'

'Not her.' Jefferson coughed. 'Yourself.' David stared at him. 'Forgive yourself first. You blame yourself too much for trusting her in the first place. It happens, son. We all trust someone so much and these exact people break that trust.'

'It's easier to forgive others, father but nearly impossible to forgive ourselves.' said David in guilt.

'Because the belief we had in ourselves had come from them who wounded us.' answered Jefferson.

'If you truly love that girl David then after every inch of being hurt you must go back to her.' David looked at his father desperately with his teary eyes. 'But don't you ever go back to her in desperation. Be a real man. Command over the love you deserve or if it is not there then go somewhere else. Don't let old good memories of that person hold you back. Such memories are not a promise that the future will be also the same with them.'

'I can be happy with someone else?' asked David naively.

'If you let yourself be.' answered Jefferson.

David nodded to Jefferson expressing his concur.

'In all this talk I forgot to ask you. Where have you been for all this time?' asked Jefferson, changing the tune of his talk.

'Brighton.' answered David.

Jeff laughed to himself, 'You so much wanted to go away from all of us that you chose the south-est place of England.' And he laughed so hard that he coughed weakly.

David came close to his father; he put his hand on his shoulder, 'Easy.' he said.

Jeff looked closely in his son's face. He looked at him like he had looked at David for the first time, when he was born on that charming evening of May 1992. Even David felt good to be near his father after a long time and he wanted to be around him every second of his remaining time.

'David I have a wish before I die.' requested Jeff in his weak voice. 'Will you approve of it?'

'What is it?' he asked like a concerned son that he always wanted to be with him.

'I want to have a beer with my son, once, before I go.' said Jefferson. David laughed and shook his head in disbelief. 'Come on. You can make an exception for your old man.'

David looked at his father's eyes and there was that desperate cry asking David to just once follow what his father believed. David fell silent and was mulling over the thought.

'This is a hospital, you do know that right? It is not allowed to bring liquors in here.'

Jefferson was frustratingly disappointed, 'Boy you are always bound by the boundaries of proprieties.' Jeff was annoyed. 'Just break free man, that's where the real fun is.'

David looked at him indifferently. Showing that it won't change his mind. 'I am not leaving this room. I want to spend every second around you.'

'Don't worry I won't die till you return. I promise you that.' David still had his indifferent stare at his father. Jeff tried again in his sad and poor tone, 'I don't want to live my last moments cowardly. I wanna live it up like a man. A man who drank and smiled at his coming death while enjoying his moment along with his beloved son.'

David sighed. 'Fair enough. Always have to be dramatic to make it in his own way.' David said to himself and stood up to get him some beer. Jefferson smiled wickedly over his victory.

'You better hold on, old man I'll be back shortly.' said David while he was getting out of the room.

Outside he saw Agatha was eagerly waiting to get into the room. 'Go. Have your time with him till I come back, mother.' David said with a coy smile at his mother and walked rapidly to the nearest liquor store. He grabbed two beers, one for Jeff and finally one for himself. He put the beer into the empty coffee cups to make it look like he is carrying coffee while he smuggles the beer to his father. Then his phone rang, he made sure that he grabbed the cup holder well into his one hand

and then with another hand he picked up the phone.

'This is David.' he said on the phone.

'It's me.' a familiar voice answered on the phone. 'Vanessa.' the girl answered.

'Hey...hi.' David was pleasantly surprised to see her call.

'I was just worried if things are better there or not. I was going to call you soon but then I thought you could be so busy at such times so I thought I shouldn't bother you with my phone call...' Vanessa said quite hesitatingly, unsure whether it is still even the right time to talk with him.

'Not at all.' answered David.

'I am not disturbing you right now, right?' Vanessa was still so hesitant.

'Well I was just grabbing a beer.' answered David.

'You started to drink?' Vanessa was so surprised.

David laughed to himself, 'Well, actually it's my old man's last wish that I drink with him once.' he answered.

Vanessa was amused with that answer, 'Looks like a real passionate man, your father.'

'He's just a dramatic man.' answered David. 'I'm telling you he just can't be without drinking. It's all his drama.' David was so happy. For the first time in a long period, he was talking about his father with someone. And the first time there was no hate but happiness.

'Looks like someone having a good time with his father.' Vanessa said.

'Yeah.' said David. 'After a really long time.'

'I'm happy for you David.' said Vanessa.

'Hmm.' David said teasingly.

'Shut up.' answered Vanessa. 'I am happy and let me be.'

David laughed heartily.

'David there is also something I have been wanting to tell you.'

'I am listening.'

Vanessa was so serene and was nervous, 'David there is someone who really likes you and probably loves you.' David thought of Jane. 'And she knows that you love someone else.' David's walk was slowed by the answer. He understood that Vanessa was talking about herself. 'And that girl knows that somewhere he also likes her but something is holding him behind. His past actually. So right now that girl is not sure what she is gonna get...but she hopes for what's best for him. But if he believes that he can be happy with her and ever chooses her...then she expects one thing from him that when he comes back to her... he comes back all of him because that girl wants all of him. So she expects that he must make his choice soon about where he wants to go because every time passes this girl's heart is breaking with insecurities and worries. At least whatever his choice may be, a clear answer would be something she still deserves.' said Vanessa almost in her crying voice. 'You understand David, right?'

David was silent for a moment. He was serious and just spoke up blankly, 'Yes. I understand.'

'See you soon David.' said Vanessa. 'And enjoy your first beer with your father. I wish you both happiness.' and she put the phone down. He was dazed with her words. Soon understanding that he was onto a very important quest he sped up towards hospital.

David had reached to the hospital foyer and now grabbed a lift to get to the hospital floor of his father's room. As he reached the floor he walked swiftly with his mind occupied in thoughts of happiness that he was gonna enjoy shortly. He was running towards the hospital room like he would run to his father in childhood. He reached the hospital room, the door was open and Agatha was sobbing so hard on Jeff's chest.

Jefferson had gone.

David was stunned with a shock. And his heart was weeping with the realization that he was cheated by his father. He hated him to ask him to go away and grab him this damn beer that he was still holding in his hands. Jeff had promised David that he would hold on till he gets back but he didn't, and the tears of pain were flooding through David's eyes.

CHAPTER 8
BOX OF OLD GIFTS

New Calton Burial Ground, around fifty people in black were gathered to mourn for Jefferson's funeral. It was an afternoon on Thursday and the sunlight was shining over the green grass of the graveyard field. Long-distance relatives, whom David never knew, had come to pay their respects and mostly Jefferson's friends from the bar had gathered in a group.

Agatha was trying strong to hold her weeping and Pamela had accompanied her, comforting her in such times. Pam looked over the coffin, there was a young boy in a black suit, wearing black sunglasses and his silk hairs were dancing in that afternoon breeze. David, he looked struck harder by this misfortune. The shock he had encountered in the hospital had not worn off yet from him. And he was extremely serene, just staring at his dead father in a coffin.

After the priest's ceremony and a couple of funeral speeches the coffin was put to the grave and David walked up to it, looked down to it for a couple of moments, realizing that his father had slept in peace in that brown coffin. He grabbed the soil in his right palm and raised his hand over the grave and after a moment released the soil which fell upon the shiny coffin. Then he walked away from it and everybody there did the same, one by one.

David had come to the car and stood there looking at everyone. People who were returning were meeting up David and asking him to look after himself and Agatha. His heart was filled up with guilt and mind was suffocating around these people he rarely met before, until Pamela came to him.

'How are you holding on David?' asked Pamela.

'I am buried in guilt that I could not even fulfill his last wish.' David answered remorsefully. 'He didn't get what he wanted even before a moment to his death. I am numbed to see how some people die with such bad luck that they aren't even allowed to live their last wish by fate.' 'I think for once to be a good father to you before HE dies was his last wish.' said Pamela hopefully.

David kept staring at her, disoriented with her answer. He took off his glasses and Pam noticed that David was just trying to hide his misty eyes from all of them. She felt so pity for him and hugged him. 'Things will be better with you David. I believe that they will.' she said.

David was quiet for a moment then he hugged back to Pam and finally allowed himself to grieve over his father's death. He cried like a teenager, battling to be strong in such a weak moment and failing to do so, everything at once, simultaneously. Pam moved her hand over the back of his head, assuring him that he is not alone. David cried off his sorrow on Pam's shoulder.

After some time he loosened his hug and looked at Pam like a little child does to his mother. 'I am sorry I was rude to you in the hospital canteen.'

Pamela smiled and wiped his fresh tears. 'It's okay David. You are my son after all.' David put lots of effort into not crying. Pam saw his struggle and said, 'You love that don't you when I call you son?'

'A lot.' confessed David.

'I miss the old days. I wish things could go back to how they were before.' said Pam.

David sniffed and looked at Pam. 'I am gonna see her.'

Pamela was confused but she hoped it was what she was thinking.

'I will come to that home and see Jane.' Pamela's face changed to bright happiness. 'Just don't hold your hopes high Pam. I don't know what is going to be my decision exactly.'

Negativity was growing over her face again but the ray of hope in her heart brought back a courageous and hopeful smile on her face. 'I hope that the decision you take will be positive David.'

David looked curiously at her, 'Positive for whom actually?'

'For me.' answered Pam. She really missed the old days and was hoping so desperately that things will go back to what they were. She needed that home what it used to be when David was along.

'Knowing that you believe in me has always given me courage. You don't know how much it means to me.'

Pam smiled gladly. 'I am so happy that after a long time you'd be coming back to that home.' said Pam. 'Jane would be so happy to know that you are coming.'

'That's the thing I don't want Jane to know about me coming there, at your home. I need you to keep it to yourself.' David was so serene and Pam thought it's better to not argue with that and she agreed to that and walked towards her car.

After a while when everyone had gone David drove Agatha to their old house. David put the car keys on the table in the drawing-room and was heading to his old room.

'David.' Agatha said. David looked back. 'Can we have a talk?' asked Agatha.

'About what?' questioned David.

'Maybe about how you are holding up to the loss of Jefferson.' Agatha said so sympathetically that it was annoying David that there can be some genuine concern in Agatha for him.

'I had talked about it with Pam. So there is really no need for that anymore.' David said and was moving back to his room.

'I always felt jealous of Pam.' These words attracted David's full attention towards Agatha that he dropped the idea of spending time alone in his room. 'We parents are often so consumed with the idea that how our children should be that we often forget how WE should be for them.' Agatha said regretfully.

Agatha sat on the sofa and David took a seat on the chair. 'I used to feel so hateful to Pam to see how you are connected with her, much more than you are to me. But I couldn't blame her for that when it was my own incapability that I never let you connect with me. I was so busy controlling you.' Agatha exhaled in regret. 'We both did you some emotional wrong. All these years we never accepted it because it was our ego that came between us.'

'Parents are also humans and they can make mistakes, I kept telling you guys but you never listened to me. It was Pam who always listened to me. I really wished that it was you who would.' David said disappointingly.

'I know and now it's too late.' said Agatha. 'Sometimes, we are really blinded in life that we fail to see the things that really matter. I was annoyed by the financial problems a lot and I didn't think about family. I just wanted to let go of all because it was getting such a burden for me but now I see the kind of life I am living is the actual burden that I am suffering.'

David scoffed and nodded in dismay, 'What is the point of it all now? Time has passed, mother. I am a grown man and as much as I truly wish to become a child again so that I can live all those things that I could not, it still won't work. Time stops for nobody. Either we value the people at the right time or regret later in life, that's the rule of life. You all made me feel stupid for holding on to the people. I really wish you could see the value of your own people and spend some time with them when there was time, instead of wasting it in a futile chase of life.'

'I am sorry David.' said Agatha bursting into tears. She was regretting her mistake. She had hurt her son. 'Could you please forgive me?' She begged desperately. She had weight on her heart. A guilt of doing wrong to someone is one of the heaviest burdens.

David looked at his sobbing mother for a while then walked up and hugged her. 'I love you mother. I always missed you. And I will always love you no matter how you treated me.' Agatha burst into more tears with those words. David loosened the hug. He sat on his knees before her, 'I wanted to hurt you.' he said. 'I wanted to hurt you as much as I can because you hurt me, mother. Because I could never accept that YOU, my own mother could hurt me. Everyone kept hurting me but despite that I still loved them, because I am really not capable of hate as you people can and certainly not leave after getting hurt.'

'That's good in you David.'

'And all of you treated it like a weakness. I thought it could be my strength but now I don't want to live my life with this burden Mother. I still don't want you in my life because the thing you did in the past was so wrong but what I can truly do for you is to forgive you for the hurt you caused me.'

The hope Agatha had that may now she would be able to restore her relations with her son was gone with the straight answer from David.

'You live the life you always wanted. You have my best wishes but now it is time for me to get the life that I always needed.' He said and was walking to his room. He stopped and said, 'And mother, you were not the only one who was jealous of bonding between Pam and I.' said David and he walked off from the drawing-room.

David spent the whole day in his childhood room thinking over the options in his life and the choices he should make.

The hardest battles are fought in the human heart and David was having one right now. There was a part of his heart who missed what he had in his past. All the good things he had with Pam and Jane, a family, a home and he was truly happy AND on the other part of his heart were the lessons he had received from his father. The practicality in life was his lesson and there should absolutely no compromise to the quality of love one deserves.

But then thoughts of Pamela had crossed his head that it's usually ego that breaks the beautiful relations in life which were true in David's life. He had seen his parents and now was getting subdued because of Pam's words.

But the thoughts of Jane and her actions that broke all this relation was also upsetting him. And with all these two different sides of his heart. He was getting mad and equally angry over himself that Jefferson was right. He should not treat himself like that. He should stand for himself despite worrying about the judgments of the people.

After getting numb of all these thoughts He finally decided to make a decision on the time when he confronts Jane tomorrow afternoon. Whatever he feels right then he would choose that and shall not look back.

A thought of Vanessa also crossed in David's head. He shook his head and punched angrily on the wall of his room.

While all these thoughts were numbing his mind, the mourning for his father in his heart was punishing him most. David was battling the worst in his heart. He missed his father. He missed him so much and could not tell anyone.

So he went to his father's room and checked out the drawers for the old album. He watched those old photos of his childhood with his father. Photographs tend to make us relive those moments of the past.

[Friday Afternoon: Jane's Home]

David rang the bell and Pamela answered the door. She was expecting him and welcomed him with a pleasant smile. 'Come in.' she said.

David was wearing a casual dress. A white shirt and a slim bottom, perfectly fit, navy blue trousers, black shoes and blue melange sweater, sleeves pulled to his mid arms and an old silver wristwatch was shining on his left wrist.

David observed the hall. Pam saw him observing the home that he was deprived of two years ago.

'There is some fragrance of old times in the air of this home.' said David.

'There would be, you have returned after all.' answered Pamela.

David walked into the home and went to the drawing-room. 'We used to watch movies here together and then have food.' David smiled, experiencing old memories before his eyes.

Pamela was getting happier to see him like this. It was giving her some hope that things might go back to what they were before.

'Ah! The bookshelf.' David saw the bookshelf he had asked Pamela to make at home. All those books he had asked to buy and read were all there on that shelf. David moved his palm over the spine of books. 'The Little Women... still your favourite?'

'Yes.' answered Pamela gladly.

'And what more do we have here?' David said while observing the bookshelf. 'Jane Austin's complete work, The Great Gatsby, Wuthering Heights...'

'That one was really painful to read.' said Pam, 'Envy, Nostalgia and Resentment.'

'Lovers could be extreme haters of each other.' said David, going nostalgic. He remembered how he and Jane became extreme haters of each other from the complete inseparable that they always were. 'Catherine and Heathcliff.' David said it like he's taking the name of Jane's and his own.

'Their own love had redeemed them from the monster that they had become.' Pam subtly tried to hint David of redemption of Jane.

David acted unheard of it and tried to observe other books, 'The Catcher in the Rye. Always loved that one.' said David playfully, 'I always felt much more like Holden in my teenage.'

Pamela had a smile on her face in response.

And there was a book that stunned David and he looked at it for a while.

Pamela saw it and spoke off, 'Anna Karenina by Leo Tolstoy, your favourite book of all time.'

David stared contemptibly at it and had tears rising in his eyes. 'Maybe my most hateful book of all time.'

Pamela got silent with that. The year Jane had cheated him was the year he had started by that very book and David related himself with the story and somewhere superstitiously blamed himself that it all had happened to him because he had started the year with that book. Nobel Alexei Alexandrovich Karenin was his favourite character from that book. And he had taken Jane as Anna and the boy she cheated him with as Vronsky and then it all added up.

'Where is she?' asked David without looking at Pam.

'In her room.'

David drew a deep breath and exhaled and walked right straight up to Jane's room.

He stood before her door. He was feeling emotional nervousness and excitement to see Jane after a long time. After a moment he gathered some courage and knocked on the door.

A dim sound of movement could be heard and David was preparing for the coming moment.

'What mom?' Jane said irritatingly and the sight of David on her door had frozen her in surprise. It took her couple of moments to process that David was actually standing right before her eyes.

The stroke of happiness and excitement had emerged from her heart that she was gonna hug him but instantly she held her arms halfway in the air and then resumed to her prior composure.

'Hello Jane.' David said looking directly into her big brown eyes. The, as usual, lively eyes looked sad like winter evening.

'David.' said Jane, still in awe.

He loved the sound of his name most when she spoke it.

For a moment they both looked at each other, lost into the battle that after all this long time now they are standing before each other. Jane was nervous but glad to see David, while he was confused with the new alien feeling he was getting.

'I'm sorry to hear about your dad.' said Jane.

David maintained his stare. 'You didn't show up to the funeral.' Despite what had happened in the past he still had expected Jane to be in the funeral of Jefferson. After all Jeff had loved Jane as his own daughter.

'I thought about coming but then I remembered what I had said back then and I thought it would be rather better if I don't visit than making things worse by my presence.'

David felt that right but still, something was going on in his heart. A search. A search for genuine care.

'How have you been Jane?' asked David. He walked into the room starting to observe objects in it.

Jane was a bit nervous and was measuring her words to be a proper response. 'Been good.' David sensed the calculated exposure in her toning and short reply. 'How come you are here David?' she was a little surprised but yet it looked like she had expected him to be there.

'To see you.' David said, looking at the black Acoustic guitar put on the corner. 'Been practicing lately?'

'Yeah. When I get nostalgic I play some songs on it.'

'Hmm.' David looked observantly at the guitar. 'I still remember our back up plan for failure.'

Jane laughed on it and there was that spark in her face for a while. 'Yeah me too.'

'If we fail to get a job.' said David. 'We'd form a roadside band and entertain people with music and earn our livelihood.'

'Classic Beggars.' said Jane with a smile on her face. David looked at her and she maintained that stare in his eyes, like they both searched something in each other, maybe their old version.

'Pam had come to see me in hospital.' said David.

'I know she told me that she saw you there. She was so happy to see you.' answered Jane.

'Were you?' asked David. That got Jane speechless. If she says yes she admits that she was wrong years ago that she wouldn't miss him and if she doesn't then she suffocates with her excitement that she just wanted to say to him how much she missed him.

'I felt good to hear that you both met.' said Jane.

'Oh! Is that so?' David hinted at her mark of jealousy. 'It's difficult to believe that, it was you two years ago who had asked us to break relations with each other. I wasn't happy with that at that time, I, in fact, hated you.'

'Mom wasn't happy either and your hatred is understandable.' said Jane apologetically. 'You both shared a beautiful bonding and I broke that.'

'Out of jealousy.' said David. He knew that Jane was somewhere jealous of David for having a good son-mother relationship with her own mother. Pam used to talk a lot about him and Jane would often speak about it on phone with David which he loved to hear and also was his usual fun to tease Jane that Pam loves him more than her.

'Yeah out of jealousy.' admitted Jane.

'You hurt people beyond measure Jane. You could be so childish and selfish but this was so cruel.'

'I'm sorry David.' said Jane.

'Sorry?' he scoffed at that word. 'Sorry doesn't fill up the chasm which your actions brought into this relation.' David was angry. 'You used a blood relation to show your power and hurt me, as if infidelity wasn't enough?'

'I was so insecure and mad at you David. You had told my mother about it to my mother.'

'I didn't have relations to maintain only with you Jane. I had duty towards Pamela too. I tried to talk out with you about the issues but you didn't care, when I saw things going out of my control only then I informed Pamela. So that she could save what we all had, even after your infidelity.'

'She was my mother.' said Jane authoritatively and soon got subdued, 'But yet she had taken your side.'

'Because she is a compassionate woman Jane.' answered David. 'Our relations were built on bonding while yours were on blood and you used that blood to show your superiority.' David was disgusted.

'I was mad at you for telling it to her. I understand that you've always been faithful to her and you did what was right. Seeing me going in the wrong direction you informed her so that you could bring me back to the right direction.'

'You understand that now?' David said in disbelief.

'We can still make it work David.' said Jane hopefully.

'Why should we?' He asked.

'I realized that you truly loved me. You truly tried everything at that time to save this relationship.' said Jane.

'Hmm. Apparently lots of people are realizing that?' asked David nagged. 'Why now?'

'I felt it at that time too but I didn't believe it. I was so angry...' David scoffed and shook his head in disbelief. 'You don't trust me?' asked Jane.

'Trust you? After everything that you've done?' David asked by looking deep into her eyes. 'But then even now I experience a lie from you.'

'What lie?' asked Jane.

'This. All of it that is happening now. Suddenly you realize my worth? Questionable.' said David. 'What did you say to me before breaking up? *This isn't working for me. This relationship, it's not what it used to be anymore. There isn't that spark that used to be in the relationship.*' he spoke out those exact words of Jane. 'Seriously that was your excuse? I was so taken aback with those words Jane, a slow realization was numbing my heart that it is also happening to me like many out there.'

'I don't know David. The relationship wasn't what it used to be.' Jane was still sure of the perception which only annoyed David more.

'Relationship was still the same love, it wasn't just enough for you.' She looked at him with eyes filled with guilt and hatred.

David continued, 'I often watched people reacting to these situations feeling wounded like they never did and I always scoffed at them thinking that they are just cowards who can't accept the change. But when it had happened to me then I had realized how devastating it was for them to realize that they aren't as valuable as they once were. This shock of realization that we started to see our worth because of someone, has disowned us from that exact worth and now we don't know what we are. Lost in the torturing questions like why did it happen? What went wrong really? Why can't it last? And there is no answer to it except the one we convince ourselves. And then that's how we go on in life, dead inside, afraid to live again.'

'I hurt you, I know.' Jane said apologetically.

'Hurt is such a gentle word for the torture you caused me, my dear Jane.' David paused and looked at her contemptibly. 'You even humiliated me for money? Can't believe that YOU could do that with me. And for what Jane? 500 pounds? That's 1% of what I earn now.' said David.

Jane walked up to David being overwhelmed with those words, 'Oh No. No. David, I just wanted to protect you from the real hurt. I had intentionally made an excuse of money that you owed me and humiliated you for that, so that you would hate me and will go away. You had always been humiliated for lack of money and I did the same.

I was so horrible but I was just trying to protect you from the worse truth that I betrayed you, David.'

He just kept looking at her, confused whether that was really her love for him or just another reverse charm that she often used.

'When a boy is young,' said David, 'He is often foolish and futile, chasing things like love. He falls in love with a girl, until his heart is broken by the exact girl. After suffering enough pain in waiting till he realizes that there is no point in waiting and then he falls in love again, the love of success and things like romantic love means nothing in that kind of life.'

Jane looked painfully at him.

'Life is a suffering and we are constantly engaged to alleviate it. While most people were busy earning money for alleviation, I however was busy looking for true love.' David stopped and swallowed the gulp of his throat. 'I lacked love Jane, not money.'

Jane started to sob so hard.

'See what you've done to me, my dear Jane. See how you have changed me.' spoke David, feeling wounded. 'Your friend Priscilla.'

'I know it was so offensive.' admitted Jane.

'SHE dared to question me. She spoke rudely, showing me that I am not your closest friend anymore? Since when the third person could speak between us, Jane? You didn't just betray my love, you also betrayed my friendship. The change Jane, how? How could you change this much?'

'David, you followed properties. I felt caged. I wanted to do lots of things in life.'

'We had decided to do them together.'

'You weren't there David.'

'I thought you understood financial problems at my home. Only if you had patience then we both would be living together now.'

'That's what I am trying to tell you, David. We can still make it work.'

'And I ask why should accept you after what you put me through?' asked David, Jane was subdued to that and kept her mouth shut. 'I was so hurting when I saw my life was scattered around. You left, father had loans on him, even mom left and you even broke my last resort, Pam. I called you damn it, to talk about what I am going through, begging you to come back, begging you to not hurt me but it was that bitch friend of yours, Priscilla, who answered the phone and didn't even allow me to talk to you. She talked to me right before your eyes that means you allowed her to behave like that with me.'

'I am sorry David. I know it's not enough...'

'Why don't you go to your sweet friend and talk to her about it. She was such a close friend, right?'

'I can't.'

'Why? Oh, don't tell me that NOW you have left her because you knew that would be my first condition.'

'It's...' Jane was hesitant. 'It's turned out that Priscilla was a real bitch, just because her own relationship didn't work out well, she spoiled mine too; influencing me that I deserve something better. Turns out she was envious of what I had. A genuine bond.'

David scoffed, 'We fell apart for the person who didn't even care for any of us.'

Jane's head fell down in shame and regret.

'You were dating that guy Harold, what happened between you two that a sudden realization made you to reconcile with me?' asked

David. 'I suspect that relationship didn't work, did it?'

'No.' Jane spoke off shamefully.

David scoffed patronizingly.

'I couldn't even believe that how could you live so carelessly after damaging my life. I mean how could people not feel anything at all knowing that because of them someone else's life is damaged.'

'I paid the price for that.' said Jane.

'Why did it break?' asked David. He wasn't interested in her self-pity.

'Harold just was using me for passing his time, to alleviate his loneliness, till he gets someone better in life.'

'That feeling stings, doesn't it?' David remarked on her for causing the same suffering in the past.

'At the beginning, he was such a nice and good guy. I felt like I am truly happy.' David nodded in dismay, as if she was truly unhappy with him before. It still hurt him. 'Then he was getting annoyed by my childish behaviour and clinginess.' Jane had a lump in her throat. 'He abused me and called me things.'

'Ah! Did he also?' David remarked again. He had called bitch to Jane at that time when he was too angry and hurt and she had made it look like David was abusive just like his own father.

'You cheated him when he was loyal to you,' said Jane, 'Why wouldn't you cheat me when the time comes. Fuck you, Jane. I am done with a slut like you.' Jane sniffed in humiliation.

'Karma.' said David. '...spares no one.'

'I am sorry David I could not understand the worth of your love then. I was so...so stupid. You have always forgiven me after my mistakes; please forgive me for the last time. I understand now how you always endured me, my childish behaviour and clinginess. You never got annoyed.'

'I was getting annoyed by that too Jane, but I concealed that annoyance because it was making you comfortable to behave with me the way you truly wanted to be. I didn't want to take that thing from you. I just wanted you to not feel shame for your mistakes or your faults when you are with me. But all this meant nothing to you.' David had tears too in his eyes. 'We think that we keep people bound to us by emotions, we can't actually, we keep people bound to us by money.'

Jane cupped her face with palm and started to sob.

'What we had was really beautiful Jane. Do you remember the gifts you gave me on birthdays? That headphone was my favourite, never allowed to touch them to any of my other friends. Because those were special, it had your touch and I didn't want someone else to touch this and contaminate it. But then you allowed yourself to be touched by someone else.' David said, trying so hard to control his weeping. He still felt that wound.

'I'm so... so sorry David.' Jane sobbed.

'You killed the purity of the relation Jane.' said David and wiped his tears with fingers. 'I kept asking, why YOU? Why did you have to be the one to damage me most Jane? It should be all other people in the world and you were supposed to redress that hurt with your love, but you used that exact love to hurt me most.' David inhaled overwhelmingly. 'You were my most-best-est friend in the world, how could you do this?' David grunted in anger. Jane would often call him her most-best-est friend. He remembered that memory and it stung him so deep. 'Do you even know how painful it is to lose the friendship, it was worse than heartbreak for me Jane.'

'I...' Jane had no words.

'You spoiled the purity of this relationship when you allowed that boy to touch you.' said David. 'I don't think this relationship will be what it used to be.'

'Oh! So you loved my body?' said Jane.

David looked at her angrily for her foolishness. 'Even if you were raped, Jane, nothing would have changed for me. I would have still loved you the same. Because your love wasn't contaminated because of that. And if that love was pure as it was, then nothing could contaminate your body. Love is connection, Jane. It's not about physicality.'

'Then why would you not give me a chance to make it work again? To give this relationship another chance?'

David thought for a moment, came closer to her, held her arms and looked into her teary eyes, 'What if the relations with that guy would have lasted?' asked David.

Jane kept looking at him blankly.

''Would you have realized then that my love for you was real?'

David had received his answer in Jane's expressions. He scoffed and laughed on himself. 'No.' he said. 'You wouldn't have understood the real worth of my love. If the relations with him would have survived then you would have always believed that you had made the right choice for yourself. And because of that, you would have never understood the worth of my love.' completed David.

Jane looked at him the way she used to when she would come before him after making a mistake, feeling guilty and making that innocent face and staring at him with those brown big eyes.

'But my sweet dear Jane, even if you wouldn't have understood the real worth of my love, still it would have the same value as it is now for you. The only difference would have been that you would not be able to see then, but that doesn't mean the love I had for you had no value.'

'David.' she grabbed his sweater to his chest and tried to hold him to stay. 'Don't go, please.'

David looked so compassionately to her and came forward and kissed her on her forehead for a long moment. Jane closed her eyes. That was the best feeling she had but lots of pain in it. Tears rolled down as she closed her eyes.

'I love you, David.' she said.

'And I shall always love that old sweet Jane of mine.' She understood that it's clear No from him. 'You deserve love and I hope you will get it but it won't be with Me.'

'Why?' said Jane helplessly.

'Because it wouldn't be what it used to be Jane.'

'We had so many good memories David. We can have more in future, then you'd be convinced.'

'No Jane. Old good memories aren't a promise of a bright new future because when you cheated me, you still had those memories but you cheated me anyway and it still breaks my heart when I think about it.' said David. 'That's why my victory is in not being affected anymore of your actions and old memories.'

She sobbed. She wept but there was nothing she could change. She felt the exact feeling of helplessness which she made David feel two years ago.

'I hate you, Jane, for robbing me of the beautiful life I could have with you. I was going to fulfill my dream because of that. You took my dream too.' said David. 'Do you even remember what my dream was?'

'To be a writer.' Jane answered serenely.

'I was going to write about our friendship, Jane. That's how I was going to show you what I truly feel for you, how much you truly meant to me. I started to write about it. I had written 140 pages in five weeks.'

This answer made her look admiringly at David.

'But then it all collapsed. I couldn't write anymore because it was all a lie. I thought I am writing about my most beautiful reality but when I couldn't live that reality anymore, I couldn't write either. But now I will. I will write about us and that's how I deal with this hatred with you.'

'So now I become the bad character in your novel?'

'No, my sweet Jane, you'll never be my enemy. You'd always be my lesson.'

'You wouldn't take your revenge then?'

'I will have my revenge.' answered David. 'It just wouldn't be what you define a revenge to be. For me, it's always going to be not like you. So you wouldn't be hated in the novel as you made people around us hate me.' Jane wiped her tears and nodded. 'On the contrary, your character will be so-so loved by the readers and I will do that, so that they still have hope for true love in their hearts.'

'Changing your reality into the book and making them all feel that otherwise than your actual reality?' asked Jane.

'I'll be scoffing at my readers for the beautiful lie they would believe in and when they'll praise your character, you will die every day, knowing that you aren't really that good, as people think of you.'

'David,' said Jane looking so painfully hopeful to him. 'Don't punish me like that, please.'

'I can't handle the pain of good memories anymore, Jane. I must disown them.' answered David.

Jane was silent for a while and said, 'What would be the name of the book based on our memories David?'

David walked up to her and brought his mouth to her left ear and whispered the name of the book. She closed her eyes, the title had hurt her even more. And he kissed her on her left cheek and headed to the door. Jane followed him, scared that now she shall never see him again.

He went to the kitchen where Pam was making coffee for him. David saw a box on the dining table. Pamela had no idea that David was into the kitchen.

'Pam.' said David.

'I was just making coffee for us.' She was so glad and had assumed that things were gone back to where they were before. She was hopeful that the sight of each other would make them come together. David remembered how Pamela always loved to make coffee for all three of them and have a talk afterwards.

She brought a mug of coffee to the dining table and said, 'See this box.' she was so excited. 'Do you remember these?'

Pamela had taken out white Sony headphones from the box.

David's favourite gift from Jane.

'Pam.' David interrupted her. 'Just sit on the chair before me, please.' Pam was nervous and blankly sat on the chair. The serenity in David was giving her signals that something is not right.

Seeing Pam's falling excitement and growing worry, David felt guilty and he held her palms on his own, like he was begging her to stop from entertaining herself into the false fantasy that she got her broken family back, like he was going to beg her about something and she was perplexed.

'You've been such an admirable woman I had ever seen. Your dedication and constant efforts only made me admire you more. But the moment I admired you most was when you talked to me in hospital. You spoke for your daughter without caring for your own dignity, because you have lots of compassion Pam.' David had tears in his eyes, he got sentimental. 'Unconditional love for your child that only makes you an angel and I was so happy to see that same compassion and love for me too.' Pamela smiled lovingly to David. 'And I am sure you will always be happy for me, for my choices. You shall always be happy for my own happiness, like a mother does for her own child.'

Pam was starting to feel the fear she was trying so hard to avoid. She looked behind David, there stood Jane in the kitchen door, looking at her with misty eyes. Jane shook her head in denial. Pamela got the answer for her rising fear and it was confirmed.

That was a shock for Pam. She really had prayed to the god that it would work but it hadn't. And now it was her eyes which were sparkling with tears. All her pretence of happiness was shattered in a moment. She looked at David, 'I know what you wanted Pam, but I should think of what I want too.'

Pam lost her efforts to hold her cry and she let her pain lose. She cried. David held her hands tighter, trying to give her some courage. He then looked at that box of old gifts. He saw all those gifts and his other favourite, a frame of a picture. Where a little boy and girl are drawn and a scribble was written on the left lower corner, *"David and Jane, best friends forever."*

'Sometimes even FOREVER ends.' said David.

And Pam started to weep harder. David stood up and brought up his left wrist ahead, there was one gift on his wrist that he had kept to himself as the souvenir of old good times.

A silver wristwatch that Jane had gifted to him.

He took it off and put it in that box ahead of him. Pam was just staring blankly to that. It was getting difficult for her to process that. Putting the last gift on that box was symbolizing the fact that David wants to close the doors of his past and keep no contacts with Jane anymore. He doesn't want anything to hold him behind because now, right in front of the eyes of Pam, he is moving on in life.

She feared that she was going to lose David, now he will break connections with her as well. Seeing to her fear David spoke off, 'You'll always be my mother and I'll always love you and nothing can change that.'

The tears were rolling down so fast and Pam was hurting so bad. David hugged her tightly and spoke. 'Home is where you are happy.' and then started to walk away with misty eyes. Pam was just looking at David, her son, walking to his own happiness, to his new home.

[La Capannina Italian Restaurant - Brighton, England]

A waitress was taking orders from a table.

'Is Table for Two available tonight?' David asked, to the familiar face.

Hearing the familiar voice the waitress was shocked a bit and then moved around to see if what she was thinking was true.

Vanessa was so happy to see David standing right before her, holding flowers in his hand. She smiled at him and was bursting out of happiness.

'I needed to take someone to date tonight, after all.' said David confidently.

Vanessa laughed and nodded affirmatively. Seeing her answer David walked right to her and held her from the waist and kissed Vanessa right into the restaurant, before fifty people. All of them clapped for them.

'Would you be my date tonight, Vanessa?' asked David.

Before she could respond to anything her father walked up with a kitchen knife in his hand.

'Oi, who are you?' a man in his mid fifty looked ferociously at him. David was stunned with that kind of gesture. He felt instant regret.

Seeing David's condition Vanessa burst into laughter and talked to her father into Italian. And then he went back to the kitchen leaving an intimidating stare to David, which had given fright to him.

'Are you sure that you don't come from the mafia family Vanessa?' David's got a lump in his throat.

She laughed and hugged him and gave him a long kiss on his chick. It was the happiest moment for Vanessa.

We all are stuck in the past at some point in our lives. Mainly because of the happiness we had in our past and it's our failure to find such happiness in our present often leads us back to our past memories. But what we truly want is to be happy again. You will get the love you always desired. Just believe that you can and it will come to your life, just like David's.

David and Vanessa got into a relationship. Their love healed each other from the wounds of their pasts. After one year of relationship, they both got married and had two sons: twins.

David was happy. He had found his love of life that lasted till the end. He wrote the book based on his friendship and love with Jane which became a best-seller, giving him recognition and fame in England.

Pamela always lived with the unfulfilled desire of bringing back David to her and this she considered her greatest failure. Reading the book of Jane & David's friendship often made her cry and nostalgic. The book remained her most favourite till the end.

Jane got married after two years and tried to be happy with the new happiness of her life but she could never truly be happy as she would have been with David.

She missed him and in order to be happy in her mundane marriage, she visited the old good memories with David.

THE END

Acknowledgment

I'd like to thank all those social media friends who had asked me to write further events, or else it would have remained just a single blog.

I'd like to thank my publishing team who guided me from time to time and helped me to bring out the best in my endeavour.

I remember once my cousin, Mandar, saying, 'What good is a story book if there are no pictures to visualize it?' It reminded me of Lewis Carroll's quote from Alice in Wonderland and I smiled to myself, somewhere feeling convinced that I should try it out if I ever publish a book. And when this book was in process to publish I had asked his elder sister, Mayuri, to draw some sketches for my book. And I am thankful that she drew them all within a short period of time.

Nothing that I shall achieve in future without the support of these two: my brother Abhijeet and my best friend Hrishikesh. They stood by me in the turbulent times, giving me courage to chase my dream. They, too, are the reason for this dream to come true.

And the last but foremost: Shikha Ma'am. When ma'am read the story the first question she asked me was, "Why is it not a book, Piyush?" and I was so glad to realize how much she really liked the story. Many had asked to publish this story including the ma'am but I clearly had no intention of publishing it. To be honest I doubted if it is even worth publishing but her utter faith in my potential has been an immense support to me. Eventually time had demanded me to publish it and Ma'am was so happy to know that I finally took the decision to publish this story. I feel so lucky that I have a teacher like her, who is constantly encouraging me to be what I really am in the world full of people who are trying to shape me according to their own expectations. This book would not have been possible without her constant support.

And finally, Thakur Sir and Rafiq Sir would be so proud now.

Piyush Thorat

Printed in the USA
CPSIA information can be obtained
at www.ICGtesting.com
LVHW020613121023
760847LV00014B/124

9 789354 275586